Esther
A Star Is Born

OTHER BOOKS BY BRADLEY BOOTH

Esther
A Star Is Born

BRADLEY BOOTH

Pacific Press® Publishing Association
Nampa, Idaho
Oshawa, Ontario, Canada
www.pacificpress.com

Cover design by Gerald Lee Monks
Cover design resources from Lars Justinen
Inside design by Aaron Troia

Copyright © 2009 by Pacific Press® Publishing Association
Printed in the United States of America

Additional copies of this book are available by calling toll-free 1-800-765-6955 or visiting www.adventistbookcenter.com.

Library of Congress Cataloging-in-Publication Data:

Booth, Bradley, 1957–
 Esther : a star is born / Bradley Booth.
  p. cm.
 Summary: When King Xerxes chooses the beautiful teenager, Hadassah, to be the new queen of Persia, she uses the name Esther to hide her Jewish identity but eventually reveals her heritage in order to save the Jewish people from annihilation.
 ISBN 13: 978-0-8163-2359-3 (pbk.)
 ISBN 10: 0-8163-2359-3 (pbk.)
 1. Esther, Queen of Persia—Juvenile. 2. Jews—History—586 B.C.–A.D. 70—Juvenile. [1. Esther, Queen of Persia. 2. Jews—History—586 B.C.–A.D. 70 3. Kings, queens, rulers, etc. 4. Bible—History of biblical events.] I. Title.
 PZ7.B646315Et   2009
 —dc22

                                     2009021503

09 10 11 12 13 · 5 4 3 2 1

DEDICATION

This book is dedicated to my sisters—Barbara, Sandy, Linda, and Janet. I admire them for standing true to the values our parents taught us as children. Today, more than ever before, Jesus needs young women like my sisters. Like Esther in ancient Persia, they have been called for just such a time as this.

CONTENTS

CHAPTER 1

Hadassah shifted the large basket on her hip and continued looking over the food items in the stalls of the Jewish marketplace. It was late afternoon, so the selection was not as good as it would have been earlier that morning. The piles of squash had been picked over, but she managed to find two dark yellow squash that still looked firm and meaty. The rainy season was coming on and the weather was turning cooler, so the season's supply was nearly gone. The cucumbers had all been gone for weeks now, but there were plenty of leeks and garlic to choose from.

After finishing her business at that stall, the girl moved to another. She measured out lentils and chickpeas and asked the vendor to tie them in white muslin cloths. She wrapped up an omer of raisins too and then picked over the dates and found exactly what she wanted—nice sweet ones without any of the bugs that some vendors allowed to crawl over the sticky fruit.

Hadassah pulled her flowing tunic tighter around her slim waist and turned to pay the vendor for the raisins and dates, when she heard a commotion from across the marketplace.

"The war is over!" a voice shouted. "Hear ye! Hear ye! The war with the Spartans is over!"

Hadassah's heart beat faster. *The war is over! This is good news!* She knew she should be heading for home and the evening meal preparations, but she wanted to hear more about the war with the

Greeks. The Sabbath would soon be here, but maybe there was still time to hear what the messenger had to say.

She quickly counted out several copper coins and handed them to the old man selling dried fruit. His scraggly beard waggled as he bowed his thanks to her and handed her a parting gift—a small package of figs, two or three in number, but the best to be found in Susa this time of year.

"Shalom!" She nodded at the old man before crossing to the other side of the busy marketplace.

The Persians had been away on a military campaign in the west for more than two years. Good reports had come back from time to time about the successes of the Persian army, and that had encouraged everyone. Often Hadassah would see the people dancing in the streets when they heard such reports, but she found it strange that bad news seldom found its way back to the royal city of Susa. *Don't armies lose battles too?* she wondered.

But now the messenger was telling the crowd it was finally over! *Thank You, Lord!* Hadassah raised her eyes to heaven in gratefulness. The crowd was growing by the minute, but she got as close as she could and stood on her tiptoes to peer over the tops of the heads in front of her.

She was glad to hear the good news—not that she really cared who won these awful battles. To her, all wars were horrible no matter who the victor was. Both the Persians and the Spartans could be brutal, refusing to go home until they had forced the enemy to surrender or else had totally destroyed them. The Persian soldiers were especially cruel, she knew, but all the stories she had heard said the Greeks were better at military strategy. She cringed as she thought of all the men who had to die in such a war. Neither side was known for mercy.

But the thing that worried her most about this most recent war was that some of her own people had been forced to serve in the war. Several young men from the Jewish congregation where she worshiped had been conscripted by the Persian army to fight in the war against the Greeks. She cared about them and their safety, and to be honest, there were one or two of them that she really liked.

But will these young men still be alive after two years of fighting? Will they come home crippled from the war, with missing arms or legs? She cringed when she thought of such a thing. In some ways, coming home with missing limbs was worse than not coming home at all. The Greeks themselves had a saying they used when sending their young men out to battle: "Come back home carrying your shield or carried on it."

That was a horrible thing to say, but Hadassah had heard that even the mothers of these young soldiers used such expressions! *Come back victorious, carrying your shield in triumph, or don't come home at all.* That's what they were saying, even if they didn't say it directly. *If you come home the loser, we'd rather you be dead, being carried on your shield by your comrades.* To lose a battle could only mean shame for everyone.

The shields the Persian soldiers used were large enough to protect their entire bodies, but, even so, men were often wounded and maimed. A man coming home with permanent injuries could not support a family or even start one. What father would want to give his daughter to someone with a missing foot or hand? Such a cripple would be an embarrassment to his family and society and would probably have to make a living by begging.

Hadassah craned her neck to get a better view of the man giving the news. The simple gray tunic he wore was torn and dirty. His black hair and beard were uncombed, he wore no sandals, and his eyes were bloodshot as though he had been without sleep for days. There was no doubt he was in mourning—and that was bad news. It could only mean one thing for anyone awaiting news from the front lines of the war. Tragedy!

CHAPTER 2

She listened excitedly as the messenger told how King Xerxes at first had several wonderful victories on the battlefield. But then, the tables had turned. In a sea battle at Salamis, a fleet of 380 Greek ships had met an armada of 2,000 Persian ships. The odds had been overwhelmingly against the Greeks. There hadn't been a chance they could win such a battle, and yet, amazingly, the Greeks had still won!

"We have tasted bitter defeat at the hands of the Greeks, and now there is no one to rescue us from them!" the messenger called out in the late-afternoon air. "Our once proud army is gone, and I'm one of the few to come home to tell the tale. We left Persia five million soldiers strong, and now return with only five thousand."

The story sounded like a fantasy, and it frightened Hadassah deep down inside her soul. *Where is God in all of this? Doesn't He care about all this destruction and death? Doesn't He want people to live?* Worse still was the possibility that if the Greek military could protect the Greek nation from the much larger Persian military, would they dare to do more? Would they come marching on Susa and the other Persian cities of the Euphrates River Valley? She tried to stop thinking of such horrible things, but the messenger continued.

Hadassah's head was spinning as she listened to the report.

The numbers were shocking and awful beyond belief. She had to pinch herself to be sure she wasn't dreaming. Xerxes had returned home, but there was no doubt he had come home humiliated.

The girl bowed her head in disappointment. If only five thousand soldiers had come home, that meant many of the Jewish young men wouldn't be coming home either. Hadassah glanced at the faces in the crowd and noticed the expressions of fear and sadness on many of the women's faces. She couldn't bear to stay and hear more from the messenger. It was all so depressing.

Besides that, she had to go home now. There wasn't a moment more to spare. The sun was getting lower on the horizon, and she hadn't finished preparations for the evening meal. Her cousin Mordecai, the man of the house, would be home soon and would want to eat. His wife, Bithiah, was out in the community, helping a family that had several sick children, so there was no telling when she would be home. With sunset and the Sabbath hours arriving soon, it was up to Hadassah to make the evening meal.

She picked up her basket of food and put it on her head. Fortunately, her waist-length hair had been braided and tied up on her head.

Hadassah was a hard worker at the age of sixteen. The hundred and one chores she did around her cousin Mordecai's home made her invaluable. Hauling water from the community cistern, going to market to do the daily shopping, weaving cloth for the basic clothes the family needed, grinding grain for the daily bread—each had given her the skills she would need to run her own household.

She was doing the work of a grown woman, and yet her skin was as soft and clear as a baby's. Her oval face and high forehead gave her a look of distinction, almost of royalty, but it was her large emerald eyes that gave her real beauty. That and the sweet innocence she wore in her smile.

Hadassah was not a child anymore. Though slender and of average height, she was now a young woman of marrying age, and it was becoming more and more evident. Mordecai knew it, Bithiah knew it. Everybody in the Jewish community knew it. Everywhere she went, people watched her. Young men in the streets followed her steps with eager eyes. Girls her age squinted at her jealously, wishing they had her perfect features. Old women in the marketplace clucked their tongues as they remembered their younger days when the energy of youth had made them flutter their eyelashes and flirt, wondering who would seek their hand in marriage.

Of course, in her usual naive way, Hadassah had no idea that her looks and charm were so appealing. Right now all she had time for was getting home and finishing her daily tasks.

She hurried down the street, picking her way through the crowd of vendors. Several times, she had to step over obstacles—cages of cooing doves, tightly rolled rugs, and children playing a game of hounds and jackals in the dust of the street. A pack of mangy dogs darted from a back alley, nearly knocking her over, but she managed to catch her basket before it tumbled off her head onto the brick street.

Hadassah began to walk fast again. What a day! The war was finally over, but at great cost to King Xerxes and the Persians. And now she had to run just to get home and fix the evening meal.

As expected, the house was empty when she arrived. A pot of lentils she had cooked earlier in the day was still warm. She placed several flat loaves of bread in a basket, cut off several slices of goat cheese, and filled a bowl with dates and raisins. Then she changed into a clean tunic and set the table for the evening meal.

CHAPTER 3

When Mordecai came home, he and Hadassah sat down to the evening meal. Aunt Bithiah still hadn't returned home from tending the sick. Between spoonfuls of lentils and mouthfuls of bread, Hadassah shared the news she had heard in the market-place about the battles with the Greeks.

"I'm amazed a soldier would come home to tell such stories!" Mordecai added. "If I were him, I'd think twice about the consequences that can come from tales that make the king look bad. That messenger is likely to feel the full wrath of the king once his message reaches the palace. You'd better be careful, Hadassah. No king likes his people back home to hear such a negative report from the war." Mordecai looked concerned. "Rulers like Xerxes would rather record history inaccurately or not record it at all. You'd think that the man in the market would know the king has his spies on every street corner."

"You mean the story the messenger brought wasn't true?" Hadassah stared at Mordecai in disbelief.

Mordecai gave her a knowing look and then got to his feet. He went to the windows and stuck his head out to look both ways, up and down the street. Then he shut the shutters to the windows, came back to sit down beside Hadassah, and lowered his voice. "Actually, I happen to know the story is true. King Xerxes and his commanding officers arrived back in Susa just yesterday, and it's all as bad as you've said it is." Mordecai lowered his voice even further. "You see, King Xerxes is a terrible strategist when it comes to planning a war. He could overcome that weakness as a king if he would just listen to his generals, but, of course, he won't. Like any great king, he goes to war with his men and then insists on running the show. I've heard that even in the face of incredible odds, he calls down the good luck of his favorite gods—Mithra, Marduk, and Nabu—and then charges ahead into battle, expecting miracles even if the odds are against him." Mordecai rolled his eyes.

"Now, Hadassah, you know that the success of any nation in battle depends on the Lord. The Most High God rules in the heavens and gives the kingdoms of men to whomever He chooses. He gives victory in battle, but also allows defeat when it can bring about His purposes among the nations of earth." Mordecai swallowed the last drop of water from his cup.

"But these kings don't know any better. They don't understand that God created the heavens and the earth and all that is in them. They don't understand that Jehovah has existed since before time began. He is in charge of the universe, and though there may be evil in this world, when it's time for God to work through His people to bring about His will, no one can stand in His way."

Hadassah smiled at her cousin fondly. He was such a man of faith. When she was with him, she felt strength in his hope and drew courage from his trust in God.

And then Hadassah had a moment to think about all the young Jewish men who had gone off to fight in the horrid Persian War. There could have been no way they had survived the bloodshed of battles by land or sea. Jerad, Amos, Sheleph, Amitiel, Merari—she had known them all for years, and now it hurt just thinking that they would never walk the streets of Susa again. Never again would they attend the special Jewish services on the holy Sabbath day. They were all gone now, dead on some battle-field; their lives wasted for nothing but Persia's vain ambition to conquer the world! Hadassah swallowed her tears to keep from crying for them. They were gone now, and there was nothing she could do to bring them back.

The sun went down, and Hadassah celebrated the coming of the Sabbath with Mordecai. It was a simple ritual. They sang a short psalm of David and then recited the most famous Judean scripture of all, a passage taken from the writings of the prophet Moses. "Hear, Oh Israel! The Lord is our God. The Lord is One. You shall love the Lord your God with all your heart, with all your soul, and with all your might." Hadassah said the words al-most without thinking. She had said them so many times that she knew she could probably say them in her sleep.

Hadassah lit a few oil lamps. "Tell me about our homeland at the time of our captivity," she begged as she settled down on her cushion beside Mordecai. She loved to hear him tell stories from long ago and far away. This was her favorite time of the week. Whenever Cousin Mordecai told stories, Hadassah felt like a little girl again.

Mordecai smiled at her. She was sixteen now and almost a grown woman according to Jewish custom, but to Mordecai, she would always be his little Hadassah.

"Many, many years ago, before you or I were born," he began, "our great-grandfather Kish lived in Judea. Those were dark times, my child. His son, Grandfather Shimei, was only a boy of about four or five, and he used to listen to your great-grandfather Kish tell him stories just like we're doing here now."

Hadassah smiled contentedly. The flames of the oil lamps burned brightly, casting shadows on the walls of their mud brick home. The firelight made little shapes of light and shadow jump and dance, bringing Cousin Mordecai's stories to life in her imagination.

"In those days, the kings of Judah had departed from the Word of the Lord," Mordecai continued. "For decades, evil kings had ruled the house of Judah until it seemed every one of them did evil in the eyes of God. Since Hezekiah there hadn't been a good one among them. They worshiped foreign gods. They sacrificed their own children to Molech and Chemosh. They even set up their abominable pagan services in the Lord's temple. And then along came King Josiah.

"Good King Josiah is what they called him in those days. King Josiah had served the Lord with his whole heart, cleansing the nation of idol worship and the false prophets that had turned everyone away from God. He repaired and cleaned the temple complex, restored the temple sacrifices, and brought back all the godly priests to serve in the worship services.

"But it was too little, too late. The nation had slid too far spiritually. When good King Josiah died, the nation fell back into idol worship. None of his sons carried on the good he had started, and with his death, the days of hope for Judah were gone."

The dim light of the oil lamps only faintly lit the small front room of their house now, but Hadassah could see a faraway look of sadness in Cousin Mordecai's eyes.

"After good King Josiah, four more kings reigned for another twenty-three years. The ten tribes of Israel to the north had already been conquered and taken away captive by the cruel Assyrians. That had been long before—nearly one hundred fifty years before Jerusalem was finally destroyed by the Babylonians. Great-grandfather Kish had been sure the kingdom of Judah would fall, too, and when it did, he wasn't surprised—terribly sad, but not surprised. The dreaded day that had been prophesied finally arrived! God's mercy could hold out no longer. Judah had to pay for its sins."

Mordecai sighed and straightened his tired back before glancing at Hadassah again. "And now it's been nearly one hundred twenty years since the powerful King Nebuchadnezzar surrounded the walls of the Holy City and took our people captive." Mordecai's face showed his sadness, and he stopped talking for several minutes.

Hadassah was quiet too. There was little to say. Her people had once been proud worshipers at the most famous temple in all of Canaan. Solomon's temple, said to be the eighth wonder of the world, was gone now, destroyed by the Babylonian army. Why had her people made such bad decisions again and again and worshiped pagan gods? Israel's God, Jehovah, was a loving God—compassionate, merciful, and just.

He didn't ask for horrendous child sacrifices or painful cutting of the body. That's what Molech and Chemosh required. They were the chief gods of the nations living along the Jordan River Valley—the Ammonites and Moabites. And the Phoenician gods, Baal and Ashtoreth, were just as cruel.

Jehovah asked only that His people come to worship Him and confess their sins. As a sign of their repentance, they were to bring a lamb to be offered as a sacrifice, or a pair of turtledoves if they were too poor to bring a lamb. These offerings represented the sacrifice the coming Messiah would one day make for His people when He died for their sins. It was the only way they could be redeemed from a world sold into slavery by the evil one, the archenemy of God's people since the days of Eden.

But the Jews had wasted their chances of being blessed as God's chosen people. They had refused to obey His words as written in the Law of Moses and the Ten Commandments given on Mount Sinai. And now, tragically, God had allowed them to be taken away captive into a foreign land.

CHAPTER 4

Hadassah stared into the yellow flames of the oil lamps, almost hypnotized by the flickering bits of fire. A frown creased her pretty forehead as she thought about the history of her people. It seemed that everyone she knew had gotten used to the years of captivity in a foreign land. "We aren't really captives anymore," some would say. "We're here by choice."

And that was true, but being in Susa, or any other Persian city for that matter, troubled Hadassah. No matter how many times she heard all the arguments and answers to her questions, she still was never quite satisfied.

"Cousin, why have we never left for the old country?" she asked wistfully. "Why didn't our family go home to the Holy Land when some of the others did?"

Mordecai brushed a moth away that had been trying to fly into the oil-lamp flames. "That's a good question, Hadassah, and I don't have a good answer. When the Persians conquered Babylon, almost immediately the new ruler, Cyrus the Great, made a decree that any Jews who wished could return to Judah."

"So why didn't our family return?" Hadassah repeated, staring into Mordecai's eyes expectantly.

Mordecai shrugged. "It's true; most of the Jews didn't take advantage of the offer. There have been three major migrations of our people back to the Holy Land." He sighed and closed his eyes. "Sometimes I lay awake at night worrying about these missed opportunities, and I must admit, the whole thing's a shame. All our people should have returned to Jerusalem when they had the chance. There's no question in my mind about that, and I wish now our family had gone. Why we didn't go is a mystery to me. For some unknown reason, my father and Grandfather Shimei stayed on in the cities of our captivity. Maybe it was the business they had begun here. You know, the family shop was quite prosperous, buying and selling imported fabric and rugs."

He glanced at Hadassah. "Maybe it was my mother and grandmother who didn't want to go. I don't know. They've all been gone now these many years. I never did get a clear answer from any of them when they were alive.

"Yes, we should have gone," Mordecai admitted sadly. "We should have returned home to the land of our fathers." He sighed again, and his shoulders slumped a little. "What's done is done, but I fear our people are going to pay for it, sooner or later."

The words made Hadassah feel uneasy. She didn't like hearing Cousin Mordecai talk this way. It was as if he were making a dark prediction about the future of her people.

At that moment Bithiah entered the door, interrupting their late-evening talk. It was plain that she was worn out from a long day of tending the sick ones in the Jewish neighborhood. As it turned out, several families with children had come down with the same illness, and she had stayed on to help them too.

Hadassah loved Cousin Mordecai's wife as if the woman were her own mother. Aunt Bithiah, as she called her, was shorter than Hadassah and had long waves of chestnut-colored hair. She had always been kind and tender with Hadassah and loved her very much, but they had their differences.

Aunt Bithiah was quiet and soft-spoken and was always reminding Hadassah to be careful about speaking her mind in a man's world. Hadassah tended to be outspoken, especially when it seemed the right thing to do. Aunt Bithiah was always obedient and submissive to Cousin Mordecai. Hadassah wasn't sure she could be like her aunt. When she married, she was sure she would have a hard time holding her tongue, especially if she ended up marrying a man she didn't particularly like. But of course, that was how things went in a world in which men made all the marriage arrangements—Hadassah was sure she had heard those words from her Aunt Bithiah a thousand times.

Unfortunately, Hadassah remembered very little about her birth mother. She and her family had lived up the Euphrates River Valley in the city of Addan. Hadassah had known only happiness during those years when she lived in a wonderful Jewish neighborhood with several uncles, aunts, and sets of cousins. But that was before the dark days of horror and death had come.

Her entire family died tragically when a plague swept through the region. Her mother and father, her four brothers and two sisters, her uncles and aunts and grandparents. Everyone had died of the disease, so there was no one left to care for her. When her cousin Mordecai heard about the epidemic, he came to Addan and found Hadassah all alone, wandering through the family courtyard.

And that was how she came to live in the home of her cousin Mordecai in Susa, one of the royal cities of the Persian Empire. Mordecai and Bithiah had no children, so they were more than happy to welcome her into their home. She had no one else in the world.

Hadassah was blessed to have been raised in the home of a God-fearing family. She loved the stories Mordecai told about God's people from times past. He was such a good storyteller, and Hadassah was full of questions. Often she would ask questions that he didn't have the answers to, but the ones about the death of her family were the hardest of all.

"Why did God let my mother and father die?" she asked Mordecai more times than she could remember.

"Sometimes bad things happen to good people," Mordecai would try to assure her. "We were not meant for suffering, but the evil one brought sin into the world, and until the Messiah comes, we must endure suffering and pain for a while. When the One who is to come makes all things new, there will be no more sadness, no crying or death, for the former things of this wicked old world will have passed away."

Finally, Hadassah blew out the oil lamps, and Mordecai shut and barred the door. A good night's sleep was what everyone needed. They all wanted to be up early the next morning to attend the Sabbath services at the place of assembly.

But Hadassah didn't feel tired at all as she lay down on her sleeping mat. There was too much running through her head. She had seen and heard too much that day, and she was sure she wouldn't sleep for hours. She remembered vividly the words of the messenger in the marketplace—the horrific details of the butchering by both armies and the incredible odds in the battle at sea—and the picture she still had in her mind of King Xerxes finally defeated.

And Hadassah loved talking with her cousin Mordecai about the history and the fate of her people. Some day she hoped to be able to go back to Judah and see the Holy City she had heard so much about. She was glad that Jehovah was a God of mercy and still wanted His people to come home to Jerusalem. Her cousin Mordecai had raised her to be a person of hope. Without hope, it sometimes seemed there wasn't really much to live for.

But there were times of tears too. Sometimes she became lonely thinking about her mother, father, brothers, and sisters. At times like this, Mordecai would put his arm around her shoulders and comfort her as if he were her real father. And in a way, he was. Hadassah would smile through her tears, trying to be brave. She loved her cousin Mordecai and his wife.

Mordecai told her many things about her mother and father, but the fragmentary memories of her childhood were growing fainter every year. One of the few things Hadassah still remembered was that her father had been a weaver, making some of the most colorful fabric she had ever seen. She also remembered helping her mother prepare bitter herbs and unleavened bread for their Passover celebrations.

Through the pain of these memories, Mordecai had tried to teach Hadassah that God is working through all the events of history. The Lord wants to comfort His people in times of need, but He also wants them to be His witnesses in the world. He wants His chosen people to proclaim the good news that Jehovah is the One True God and that He will one day come to deliver them from their sins.

Hadassah turned on her mat and closed her eyes drowsily. The faint sounds of night drifted in through her window—a baby crying in the night, the tinkling of wind chimes on someone's upper balcony window. They were all muffled sounds now, wafting in on the night wind. Hadassah was drifting into slumber, shutting everything out but the words she had chanted at sundown that very evening. "Hear, Oh Israel! The Lord is our God. The Lord is One. You shall love the Lord your God with all your heart, with all your soul, and with all your might."

CHAPTER 5

The next day, Hadassah attended the Sabbath services with Mordecai and Bithiah. When they arrived, Hadassah and Bithiah sat with the other women on one side of the meeting room, while Mordecai sat with the men. They all sat cross-legged on the floor while they waited for Asaph, a local Jewish scribe, to read from an ancient scroll written by the prophet Moses. Some of the men and women were dressed in the dark garments of mourning. Hadassah knew many families had lost sons in the war, but others were still waiting for official word from the palace.

Hadassah glanced shyly toward the men's section and noticed with surprise that Merari was there sitting among the men. He was alive! He had returned from the war in the west against the Greeks, after all. *When had he returned home and had other young Jewish soldiers come with him, alive and well?* She hadn't heard anything about it in the marketplace the day before. Surely information like that would have traveled like wildfire through the Jewish community of Susa! It must be that he had returned just the day before—or perhaps even the previous evening. She tried to keep from staring at him. It would never do for Merari to think she was excited to see him. After all, he was really not her type.

Hadassah turned her attention to the reader as Asaph stood to his feet. He rolled out the scroll on the wooden table in front of him and then cleared his throat.

"Jehovah will establish you as His holy people if you keep the commands of the Lord your God and walk in His ways. . . . Then all the peoples on earth will see that you are called by the name of the Lord, and they will fear you. . . . The Lord will make you the head, not the tail." *Are these words still for the Jews now, in the city of Susa, almost one hundred twenty years after we have been taken captive to a foreign land?* Hadassah wondered. It didn't seem possible that the words could be true, but the promise was there, staring up at them from the scroll on which it was written. Words written on clay tablets would be more permanent, and sheets of Egyptian papyrus were cheaper to make, but scrolls like the one from which Asaph was reading were made out of calfskin or lambskin that could be rolled up and carried anywhere. And, of course, it didn't really matter what the words were written on. The Word of God was important to the Jews everywhere, no matter how or where it was written.

Hadassah thought some more about this. She knew that God's Word, as written in the scrolls of the prophets, was holy, and like God, these Scriptures could stand the test of time. The question was, Did the messages from the prophets mean the same thing for God's people now as they had so long ago before the dark days of captivity? Were the Jews still God's chosen people, and did God still want the Jews to be His light to all the world, or did God now have another plan?

In the old days of David and Solomon, the nation of Israel had been incredibly wealthy. It had been obvious that God was blessing them because they were living the way God wanted them to live. They were keeping the Sabbath holy. They were making pilgrimages to the Holy City of Jerusalem at least three times a year to attend the religious holidays. They were remembering to pay their tithes and offerings to show that they recognized God as the One and only True God, the Creator of heaven and earth.

Cousin Mordecai said God could afford to bless them because He knew they were not using the blessings to dishonor Him.

But what did God want from the Jews centuries later? What was His plan for them? Should they be going back to Judea and Jerusalem now to carry on as God's people there, just like they were supposed to do before the captivity? Or did He want them to be His missionaries in foreign lands, such as Babylon, Persia, and Media?

After the service, Hadassah noticed several young men looking her way, but none of them were appealing to her at all.

And then there was Merari. He kept smiling at her, but his gaze made her feel uncomfortable—as if she were on display. It made her feel as if she were one of the animals in the marketplace being paraded around so the farmers could bargain for it.

Self-consciously, she stepped closer to Mordecai and took his arm. Right now he was more than just a father figure to her. He was like a big brother, a protector of her honor, and the one who would be sure that the young Jewish men in the community would treat her with the respect and courtesy women deserved. Mordecai had taught her that from an early age. That she was a daughter of God, was important, but so was her need to be a virtuous young woman. She needed to be a girl the young men could respect. She needed to be able to look in the bronze mirror in her room at night and feel good about herself.

Like King Solomon had said long before, she wanted to be worth more than rubies. She wanted to be a capable wife who could make incredible things with her hands, things such as tapestries and clothes of fine linen. She wanted to be able to run an estate and yet still have time to help the poor and needy that lived near her. When she finally did marry, she wanted her future husband to admire and trust her and see her for all the beauty she possessed inside.

But Hadassah did not truly understand how incredibly attractive she already was on both the inside and the outside—and it was just as well. To be aware of such things might have made her vain and conceited, and in her heart, that was something she had never wanted to be. More than anything else, she knew it was important to be respected and admired for having godly qualities. These were things Aunt Bithiah had taught her, and she wanted them for herself too.

Some evenings by the light of a lamp, Bithiah would brush Hadassah's long flowing locks. The two of them would talk about all kinds of things, such as how much the fruits and vegetables should cost in the market and what a good loaf of bread should taste like.

But more often now, they were talking about what a girl should be like if she wanted to make herself really attractive from the inside out. Things such as not being argumentative and smiling more, leaving people guessing as to what she might be thinking. And beginning her day with God so that she could become pure and godly. That was the only real way to become the perfect girl for her future husband.

Thinking about marriage frightened Hadassah. She didn't really feel ready to get married, but then again, what girl in the Jewish community ever did? Some girls married as young as fifteen years of age, and the thought of such a thing made her all queasy inside. She didn't feel ready to run a home of her own or to have a crying baby to take care of every waking moment.

Elkanah, one of the Jewish elders, stopped to talk with Mordecai, so Hadassah released her grip on her cousin's arm and stepped away. She liked Elkanah and had known him since she first came to live in Susa. He was old enough to be her father, perhaps even her grandfather. Her mind wandered to other things as she heard Cousin Mordecai invite Elkanah to come for the evening meal.

On the way home, Hadassah asked Mordecai questions about the passages of scripture Asaph had read. "I was wondering," she began, "why the scribes at the Sabbath services don't speak of the prophecies that tell about the return of our people to Judah. I mean, if we're still God's chosen people and Jerusalem is still the Holy City of our people, why not talk about it? It's the one message we have from the prophets that seems to bring us hope."

"Well now, that's a good question. Maybe," Mordecai hesitated as though he wasn't sure Hadassah would like his answer. "Maybe—it's because most folks don't really want to return home anymore."

"Not return to Judah! Why not?" Hadassah was shocked.

"Well, the journey is no holiday trip—that's for sure. It would be a tough one and would probably take at least four or five months of steady travel. It would be filled with dangers from thieves and bandits along the way too." He raised his eyebrows at her. "Then, too, I think most folks enjoy it here. Life is easy for them. We talked about that last night. Remember?"

"I know what we talked about last night," Hadassah replied as sweetly as she knew how, "but I still think they should be talking about the things that make us Jews. We're different from other people here. We worship only one God. We sacrifice only specific animals, and we keep the seventh day holy, which is all the more reason why we shouldn't be here! We should be back home in Jerusalem with our own people!"

Mordecai glanced at her as they turned the last corner toward home. This was a new thing to hear the young girl talking about the prophecies of the prophets. Young men talked about such things sometimes, but girls usually kept quiet. He grinned at Hadassah, but didn't know quite what to say. Finally, he said the only thing he could say. "You're right, Hadassah. I can't deny it. I guess I'll have to ask Asaph that question myself. Maybe he'll have better answers for you than I have."

CHAPTER 6

All that afternoon Hadassah enjoyed the quiet Sabbath time with Mordecai and Bithiah. They ate the noon meal under the grape arbor in the courtyard and then sang a few songs from the writings of David. Mordecai could play a lyre and was teaching Hadassah how to play a reed flute. Already she was getting pretty good at it, and today the two of them were making wonderful music to sing by. Later some of the other Jewish families even stopped by to sing with them.

After a while, though, Mordecai got out one of the scrolls he had borrowed from the meeting place that morning. Lending out the precious scrolls of the Torah wasn't something that was usually allowed, but since Mordecai was a scribe himself, everyone trusted him. After all, if he lost a scroll or somehow damaged it, he could always make another copy. That's what he did for a living in the royal archives at the palace.

The scroll was very old, taken from a collection of ancient Jewish records housed in the temple in Jerusalem before the Babylonian captivity. In the scroll were stories of the famous prophets such as Elijah, Elisha, and Isaiah who tried to bring the people back to God.

Hadassah sat amazed and inspired as she listened to Mordecai read how the prophets of Baal had been defeated on Mount Carmel, how Elisha had used God's power to make an ax head float, and how an entire army of Assyrians had died in one night from a plague.

There were stories of kings in Israel and Judah. Some were good kings, but most of them were bad. Hadassah's heart grew heavy as she thought about how good God had been to her people, bringing them out of slavery in Egypt and helping them settle in Canaan. But sadly enough, before many years had passed, Israel began worshiping idols of wood, stone, and gold like the pagan nations around them did. When they strayed further and further from the kind of people God intended them to be, He finally withdrew His blessings and protection from them, leaving them to the mercy of their enemies.

Those were the kinds of stories Hadassah enjoyed. If no one was reading them to her from the scrolls, she could read them for herself. That was one of the luxuries of living in the home of a scribe. Mordecai had taught Hadassah how to read and write, something very few girls knew how to do.

Near sunset the guests left, and then Elkanah, the Jewish elder, stopped by the house and was invited in. While Mordecai and Elkanah visited, Hadassah brought a basin of water to wash Elkanah's dusty feet. She had been having so much fun studying the ancient writings that she almost forgot Elkanah was going to come for a visit.

Now she hurried to the back room to help Bithiah with the meal preparations. As usual, when a guest was coming to dine, Bithiah and Hadassah tried to prepare the best delicacies in the house. This time it was a salad made from leeks, cucumbers, and chickpeas, and, of course, the main staple of every Jewish table—bread and goat cheese.

After the meal, Hadassah helped Bithiah clean up. From the back room, she caught snatches of the conversation between Elkanah and Mordecai and heard familiar words such as *betrothal*, *dowry*, and the name *Merari*. However, when she heard her own name being mentioned, she had to wonder. Was she being bartered for in a marriage proposal? Many of her friends had already received proposals for marriage just like this. Young Jewish men in the community had come with their bride price, with the most desirable girls usually going to the highest bidder.

Was this to be Hadassah's fate too? And so soon? She knew she should probably be thinking about marriage. All girls did sooner or later, but in her heart, Hadassah knew this was not the right time or the right man.

Hadassah went to her room earlier than usual. She decided to read from a scroll of history Mordecai had lent her, but she had a hard time concentrating. Crickets were chirping, and she was tired. A light evening wind rustled the leaves of the mulberry tree just outside her window, and through it all she could hear the voices of the two men droning on into the night.

Was she right in assuming that the men were discussing her marriage plans? It certainly sounded like it. Merari's father was an influential man in the Jewish community of Susa. He wasn't wealthy enough to pay off the king and keep his son out of the war, but he was a man with connections. And Merari was a handsome young man, but that wasn't enough for Hadassah. He might be handsome, but she had never found him appealing. He talked about himself all the time and wasn't polite or respectful to the girls in the Jewish community. As far as Hadassah was concerned, he was vain, arrogant, and worst of all, ungodly. From what she had heard, Merari had a reputation for crude language, and that alone added his name to Hadassah's blacklist. Maybe Mordecai didn't know it, but Hadassah knew it, and that was enough for her.

She heaved a tired sigh. She was weary from entertaining folks all day and tired of thinking about something she had no control over. It seemed so wrong that she could be married off to someone she didn't love or even like. No matter what the grown-ups thought, it wasn't right. She couldn't imagine that God had ordained it should be that way.

Hadassah finally blew out the flickering oil lamps and lay down on her floor mat. It wasn't late, but tomorrow was another day. Maybe then she'd find out more about Cousin Mordecai's plans for her. For the time being, she just wanted to put it all out of her mind and go to sleep.

Somewhere in the night, Hadassah dreamed she was getting married, but through all the tedious details of the dream, she never did manage to see the face of the young groom. And then she awoke with a start of relief to find it was all a dream. With the sun streaming in her window, she suddenly remembered the events of the night before.

CHAPTER 7

At the morning meal, Hadassah studied Mordecai's face, but her cousin gave no hints about the conversation with Elkanah the night before. Over a fig and a bowl of leben, Hadassah tried to ignore Mordecai's obvious silence, but there was no way to hide the tension she felt. Finally, she could contain her impatience no longer.

"What did Elkanah want last night?" she asked boldly, guessing what the answer would be. Then she realized that she had overstepped her bounds as a young girl in the home, and lowered her eyes. "Please," she added more politely, "I overheard my name being mentioned. Was it about a marriage proposal?"

Mordecai stared at Hadassah. He said nothing, but Bithiah spoke sharply, "Hadassah! That was uncalled for! You had no right to be eavesdropping like that!"

"I know," Hadassah's voice fell, "but I couldn't help it. I was just around the corner in the next room! And besides, they were talking about me. Don't I have a right to know about something that has to do with me?"

Bithiah's eyes narrowed to slits. "Well, no, actually, you don't. The men make all the arrangements for anything that has to do with your future husband."

"So you *were* talking about me and a marriage proposal! I knew it!" She turned to Mordecai and rolled her eyes in exasperation.

"Honestly! Must you choose Merari, son of Bicri? Please, Cousin! I can't stand Merari!" Hadassah was raising her voice again.

"Hadassah! That will be quite enough!" Bithiah shook her finger at the girl. "You are beautiful, and you are intelligent, but you are stubborn too! Merari is a good man! He's at least ten years older than you and will provide for you well. He's brave and a hero, too, just back from the war in the west with the Greeks. Do you think God has something better in store for you than this?"

"Than Merari?" Hadassah kept her eyes on Mordecai. "Please, Cousin. Anyone would be better than Merari!" She knew that Mordecai was her only hope. If she was going to get any sympathy, it was going to have to come from Cousin Mordecai. Right now, Aunt Bithiah was being no help. Cousin Mordecai seemed to understand Hadassah better than Aunt Bithiah did. Or maybe it was just that he had a soft spot in his heart for her. After all, he did have a habit of saying she was still his little girl.

But Mordecai was the one making all the marriage arrangements. Would he care enough to listen to her this time? She wanted to be respectful, but she didn't feel like she could stand by and just let this thing happen!

"Merari is too arrogant, Cousin! He's too full of himself!" Hadassah's eyes were wide. "In our marriage, there would be no room for anyone but him!" She knew she had to keep going before she lost the courage to say what needed to be said. Making her own case was the best thing she could do right now. No one else knew exactly how she felt. "I know Merari comes from an important family," she added, "but I can't live with someone like that! I want a home where God comes first!"

After these words, Hadassah was silent. Mordecai drummed his fingers on the table and looked out the window to the garden beyond. Hadassah could feel Bithiah's disapproving eyes on her, but she kept her focus on Mordecai.

"When did Merari arrive home?" she asked, trying to change the subject a bit. "And how is it that he managed to arrange for a deputy to draw up the marriage proposal so soon?"

"He came home the same day the king did, but was recuperating in his father's house," Mordecai said, not looking at Hadassah. "And Friday he saw you in the marketplace, but he said you were in such a hurry he never even got to say Hello to you." Hadassah said nothing; her eyes were focused on the floor again.

"So when he got home Friday afternoon, he and his father went to see Elkanah to ask if he would help arrange the details of the betrothal. And—what you saw here last night was the first steps toward such an agreement."

Mordecai continued staring out the window. "According to Elkanah, Merari came home fully expecting you to already be married. But when he saw you in the marketplace, he could tell by the clothes you were wearing that you are still unmarried. To put it simply, he couldn't believe his good fortune. That's when he hurried home and spoke to his father. I think he knew he couldn't afford to wait even one more day to stake his claim."

Cousin Mordecai smiled sheepishly. "Actually, to be perfectly honest, I think he probably thought you'd welcome him home with open arms, proud to become his wife. After all, he is a war hero, coming back as one of the few survivors of the war."

Hadassah remained quiet and said no more. She figured she had said enough. Her silence would probably do more for her now than adding words to the little speech she had already given.

All that day, Hadassah worried about the discussion at the morning meal. But when evening came and they talked no more about it, she began to relax a little. *Surely Cousin Mordecai won't marry me off to someone I don't like. He loves me too much for that, doesn't he?* The two of them had always been close. At thirty-eight, he was over twice her age, but that had never come between them, and now she knew he'd do the right thing. He would listen to her and call off the proposal for her betrothal and marriage to Merari. She was sure he would.

And that's exactly what he did. The next morning, he came to the morning meal with a twinkle in his eye and the faintest bit of a smile on his face. "You are now officially a free girl again," he announced as he ate the barley cakes, leben, and citrons Bithiah had set out for him.

"Oh, thank you, Cousin!" Hadassah jumped up and threw her arms around his neck. She gave him a kiss on his right cheek, and then on his left. "I love you so much!" And with that she hurried off to get ready for the tutor who came each morning to teach her Aramaic and mathematics.

CHAPTER 8

One evening later that week, Mordecai came home with some very interesting news. King Xerxes was staging a beauty contest all up and down the Euphrates and Tigris River Valleys. But this was to be no ordinary contest—it was a competition in search of a new queen.

"It's about time he got around to finding himself a queen," Bithiah laughed, as Mordecai shared the details around the evening meal.

Mordecai scratched his dark beard. "Let's see. He threw that big holiday bash. And then he was gone on military campaigns into Mesopotamia all the way to the Greek isles. He fought several battles by land, and then pushed west into the Great Sea. So it has been a while."

Hadassah got a funny look on her face. "I never did figure that one out. Throwing a party for six months seems pretty boring to me. I get tired of eating after just a week of celebrating at one of our typical wedding feasts here in the Jewish community."

"Me too." Mordecai grinned like a little boy. "I can eat a lot, but enough's enough. After a week, every sweet cake looks the same. Every piece of goat meat tastes like the one before it. But you know how these Persians are. They like to impress one another, and the whole idea behind the six-month feast was to do just that. Wow all the generals and government diplomats with a fantastic display of wealth and power! That way no one would second-guess the king's decision to wage war with the Greeks, even if the Greeks are better warriors."

"And they are!" Hadassah laughed nervously, and then quickly added, "I shouldn't treat it like it's a joke. Scores of our own young men died in that war, just because the king was stupid enough to—"

"*Shh!*" Mordecai put his hand over Hadassah's mouth. "You'd better rethink that one! And while you're at it, you might want to speak in lower tones too." He glanced toward the closed windows and doors of their home. "You never know where spies for the king might be lurking."

Hadassah ducked her head guiltily. "Sorry."

Mordecai shook his head and rolled his eyes. "Honestly, Hadassah, one of these days you're going to get yourself into real trouble. I mean, even Queen Vashti couldn't question the king! When he said 'Dance,' she had to dance or suffer the consequences! What makes you think a little Jewish maiden like you is going to stand a chance when criticizing the king?"

"If I have to dance to please a man, I'll take my chances!" Hadassah blurted.

"And maybe die for it!"

"OK, OK." Hadassah silently mouthed the words.

"Mordecai's right," Bithiah spoke for the first time during the meal, "but I'll have to admit that I was thinking the same thing as you, Hadassah!"

"I'll bet you were." Mordecai bowed his head. "Honestly, Bithiah, I never know which way you're going to go on these things!"

"No? Well think about it, Mordecai! I mean, really now! Having to parade myself around in front of the king at his party and dance for him and his drunken cronies is not my idea of respect, or royalty either! She's the queen! If the king wanted someone to dance for him, he could get one of his dancing girls to do it! Why did he have to call the queen in and embarrass her like that and so late at night too? She wasn't that good of a dancer anyway, from what I hear. And he was too drunk to know what he was asking anyway. He was just showing off in his macho way." Bithiah rolled her eyes now too.

"Well, I guess she was pretty much thinking like you, right now, Bithiah. Which is why she was booted out of the royal palace and the harem in one swift move by order of the king."

"You mean, by order of that bunch of hyenas he calls his court advisors—Carshena, Shethar, Admatha—the whole bunch! They were just afraid that women like me would rise up everywhere and try something like that on their husbands!"

Mordecai cringed at the sound of such harsh words by his wife. "Good woman, fortunately we are in the privacy of our own home; if someone heard your criticism, you might be in danger."

"So, whose idea was it to have a beauty contest?" Hadassah could feel the tension in the air and changed the subject again.

"Probably Prince Haman," Mordecai shrugged, "or any one of his other advisors."

"Who's eligible?" Bithiah had calmed down some by now.

"Well according to the proclamation I saw being written at the palace today, I think any young maiden can qualify."

Bithiah raised her eyebrows. "You mean the young maidens don't have to be of royal blood?"

"Evidently not."

Hadassah kept looking from Cousin Mordecai to Aunt Bithiah, and then back again. Lots of exciting things happened in the royal city of Susa, but this topped anything she had heard of lately—except the stories she heard about the war with the Greeks, of course.

"So how will they run the competition?" Bithiah was asking all the questions Hadassah herself was thinking.

"I guess royal courtiers will be sent to every major city to post the proclamation so everyone can see it. On a given date, the elders or public officials of each city will be asked to bring all eligible maidens to the city gate. There court officials will examine each girl, and then take the finalists back to Susa to be inspected by the king himself."

Such a contest would be interesting to follow. Reports every day in the marketplace would be very exciting! Any news that was considered important at all ended up there, to be told and retold by every woman in the Jewish community.

Hadassah could hardly imagine what it would be like to be part of a beauty contest! Such a thing seemed impossible for young Jewish girls. Being paraded around for everyone to look at would be embarrassing and completely out of the question. Jewish girls married only young men from inside their religious community, so why worry about some beauty contest in which the winner would become the queen of a pagan king?

Hadassah helped clear away the evening meal and then excused herself to go to her room. She had studied her lessons enough for the day, and now she wanted to just read. She knew she wasn't like most of her friends. Jewish girls had to work pretty hard helping do the family chores—going to the community cistern to bring water, making bread every day, and shopping at the marketplace to buy the needed food items for family meals. During any spare time these girls had, they usually wanted to daydream about their future and fill a dowry chest with gifts the women in the community would give them at their betrothal and wedding.

But not Hadassah. She would rather learn more about the world around her than daydream, and reading was just one of the ways to do it. Most of her friends couldn't read or write, but thanks to Mordecai, Hadassah could already read Hebrew and Aramaic. Literature was her favorite subject.

She enjoyed studying the writings of Moses and songs from the legendary King David, and Solomon, the wisest of the wise. But she also liked studying the ancient historical writings of Babylon and Persia. Tonight she opened one of the scrolls Cousin Mordecai had brought home for her from the royal archives. It was a famous Babylonian story about Noah's flood called the *Epic of Gilgamesh.*

She read by the light of oil lamps for quite some time and then finally put the scroll back in its place on her reading table. Before she lay down on her sleeping mat, she knelt to pray by the open window facing west toward Jerusalem. Talking to God like this was something her Cousin Mordecai had told her she should do every night before she went to bed, and tonight was no different.

"Oh, God of my fathers," she prayed. "I'm just an ordinary Jewish maiden, but I pray that You will use me to do great things for You someday."

CHAPTER 9

The next morning when Hadassah went to the public cistern to bring home the daily water supply, she heard the local girls talking about the beauty contest being conducted at the royal palace.

But from what she could tell as she waited in line, they knew little more than what Cousin Mordecai had already told her: King Xerxes was sending his courtiers in search of beautiful young maidens throughout the Persian Empire, hundreds of girls were being interviewed in cities all up and down the Euphrates and Tigris River Valleys, and the final contest would be held right in Susa.

Later that afternoon while Hadassah was at the Jewish market doing the shopping, she heard more—beauty and intelligence would both be considered, and the king would have the final say, of course, in finding the lucky girl to be chosen as queen.

None of the information at the market was new. Mordecai had said it all back home, but it was fun hearing people talk about it on the street just the same. The local Jewish women in the marketplace saw Hadassah and asked if she was getting ready to go to the palace for the contest too.

"Me?" Hadassah glanced at the women in surprise. "Why me? They're not going to be interested in me." She tried to ignore the women as she sorted through the fruit at the vendor's stall.

"Why not?" a stout old woman asked Hadassah.

"Because—because I'm just a common Jewish girl. Why would they want me?" It was getting harder to pretend the conversation didn't bother her. Hadassah measured out some lentils and chickpeas.

"Well, that's what they want! Young maidens!" another busybody gave her a look up and down. "Who do you think you are fooling? Don't act all innocent, like you haven't a clue what we're talking about! You're a beauty, and you know it!"

"Gorgeous is more like it!" another added, rolling her eyes sarcastically. "I'd give anything to be in your place!"

Several more women had gathered around now. They were all well past their prime, and their faces showed the hard work and worries of life that were moving them quickly toward old age. But it was obvious they weren't too old to gossip. "Go on, admit it!" they all chimed in. "You know you've got as good a chance of winning that contest as anyone around!"

Hadassah's eyes flashed. "Well, I'm not interested!" she blurted, packing the last of the pomegranates and citrons into the bag she had brought along. She snatched up the bag and pushed her way through the circle of women. They were making her feel very uncomfortable. Right now all she wanted was to get away from their stares and clucking tongues.

"You won't have a choice, young lady!" one of the women called after her. "The king's courtiers will come calling, and when they do, you know you'll be summoned just like all the other beauties in the kingdom."

She ran all the way home. It was almost as if she were trying to outrun the women's words in the market. When she arrived home, no one was there, so she began preparations for the evening meal. First, she stoked the charcoal fire in the clay oven. Then she diced up some leeks and garlic and stirred them into a pot of lentils that had been simmering since she left for the market. Fresh flat barley bread and slices of goat cheese made the meal complete. It was the month of Kislev, the time of year for cool weather, so this meal was perfect.

Everyone was late getting home. While she waited, Hadassah got out her needlework and put in some time on a project Bithiah wanted her to add to her dowry chest. As Hadassah sewed tight little stitches on the fine linen garment, her mind went back to the news of the beauty contest. Would the king's royal courtiers really come looking for her? The very idea was exciting and terrifying at the same time.

The women in the marketplace had told Hadassah that her olive complexion and large emerald eyes would make her a likely candidate for the contest. But Hadassah knew nothing of these things. Raised in a home where physical beauty was second in importance to character, she failed to compare herself to other girls. Mordecai had taught her well and reminded her often that kindness to others and a sweet smile should be of more value than all the outer beauty in the world. Her slender waist and long raven hair were gifts, he said, but a shining personality and heart devoted to God should be a girl's most stunning qualities.

With no guests present at the evening meal, Hadassah and Bithiah ate with Mordecai, but Hadassah said little as was the custom for women at the meal. Between bites of bread, Mordecai told about his day at the royal archives, but eventually the talk turned to details of the royal search for a queen. Hadassah sensed he was making small talk instead of saying what was really on his mind.

When Hadassah finally got up to clear away the evening meal, Mordecai asked her to stay for a bit. "How much do you know about the search for a new queen?" he asked solemnly.

"Not much," she admitted. "Only the little bit I hear in the marketplace, and of course, what you've shared at home."

"Well, Bithiah and I have been talking about you, and we can no longer deny what everyone has been telling us all along." Mordecai's voice was calm. "We're sure now that the king's courtiers will be coming for you any day. You have many attractive qualities, and they won't miss that. Likely as not, you're already on their list. A young woman of your delicate beauty is quite uncommon." He stared at her large emerald eyes. "There's probably not a more beautiful maiden in all of Susa, if I do say so myself."

"Oh, please!" Hadassah was blushing now. "You're my cousin, so you have to say that."

Mordecai shook his head. "They know where you live, and they'll come for you. It's just a matter of time, now. In fact, I'd say the chances are high that you'll become a finalist in the contest. If that should happen, your life would change overnight, you know."

Hadassah shook her head slowly. "A finalist? What would happen then?"

Mordecai's voice grew soft. "You'd probably become a part of the king's harem."

"The king's harem?" Hadassah's eyes grew wide. "You mean I'd become one of his wives?"

"Probably."

"I'd rather not—if I have anything to say about it."

"I'm sorry," Mordecai said tenderly, "but it doesn't work that way, Hadassah." He laid his hand on her arm. "When the most powerful man in the world orders you to come to the palace, you go—no questions asked."

Bithiah came to sit down beside the wide-eyed girl. "It's all quite exciting," she tried to assure the girl. But Hadassah noticed a tear in her eye, and Bithiah's voice trembled as she added, "I'm very happy for you."

"Hey!" Hadassah shook her head. "I'm not even in the beauty contest yet, and you two already have me married off to the king." She tried to reassure them, "Everything's going to be just fine. You wait and see. This time next month, I'll still be going to the public cistern to get the water. I'll still be running errands to the marketplace, just like any other Jewish girl in our community."

Mordecai and Bithiah exchanged weak smiles, but Hadassah never noticed. She was already up and off to her room to spend time on what she loved doing most: reading some more.

All that evening while she read, Hadassah thought about her conversation with Mordecai and Bithiah. This whole thing with the royal beauty contest was getting a little bit crazy! Exciting as it might seem, she didn't want to think about what could happen. *Is there a chance that the king's officers really might come for me? Is it possible that some wild turn of events could land me in the competition?* She had never even thought about what it would be like to be in the palace because she had never wanted to be there.

CHAPTER 10

Hadassah set out a basic meal the next morning as usual—barley cakes, some leben, and a few figs and pomegranates. She was still thinking about her conversation with Mordecai and Bithiah the evening before. Try as she might, she could not shrug off the feeling that the simple days of her childhood were soon to end. At just sixteen years of age, it was time for her to grow up. The thought that she might be part of a beauty contest at the palace was a bit exciting, and the idea of becoming a wife was—well—it was all very mind-boggling.

Hadassah didn't know the exact age of the king, but she had heard he was in his late thirties like Mordecai. He was also said to be quite athletic and very handsome. To be married to someone more than twice her age seemed odd and very unromantic, but then, Jewish girls often married men twice their age. Sometimes, it was because the men could afford to pay a good bride price. Sometimes, it was simply because they were already making a very good living and could provide for a young wife.

The whole thing was unattractive to Hadassah. She dreamed that she would marry for love but knew that romance wasn't up to a girl. Marriages were arranged by men.

No one was talking at the morning meal, so Hadassah ate her figs and leben in silence. And it was just as well, with all the mixed emotions and ideas going through her head. The possibility of being forced to participate in the beauty contest just didn't seem real! Soon she would wake up to find it was all a dream.

But as Hadassah looked toward the open window, she could hear the morning birds singing. She could see the fleecy clouds scudding past in a deep-blue sky. This was no dream. She was already wide awake. Dawn had come, and with it the stark reality that this might be the day the royal courtiers would come looking for her.

"I think you should take a Persian name," Mordecai said quietly, as he brushed the crumbs of barley cake off his lap.

Hadassah jumped in surprise at the sound of his voice.

"When they come to add your name to the list of eligible candidates, you must not use your Jewish name," he said slowly.

Hadassah struggled to focus on what he was saying and then finally found her voice. "Why not?"

"Well, for one thing, we Jews are foreigners in Susa. In the court of Xerxes, Jews aren't a favored race. Under the earlier kings, Cyrus and Darius, things were different, but now there are many officials at court who hate Jews. Haman, a high official in the royal court, is one of them. And besides all this, Haman doesn't like me personally," Mordecai confessed. "He never has, and I'm sure it's because he knows I'm a Jew."

"But why doesn't he like Jews?" Hadassah stopped eating. "What did we Jews ever do to him?"

"Well, from what I've read in the royal archives, Haman descended from a Canaanite king in the days of Samuel the prophet. His ancestor was Agag, king of the ancient Amalekites. You know the story. Anyway, I think he has something against all Jews for the sake of pure revenge."

Hadassah stared at Mordecai in surprise. "The lengths people will go to hate," she sighed.

"Which is precisely why I'm worried about your identity in

the palace," Mordecai nodded. "I would hate for Haman ever to have an opportunity to take out his frustrations on you because of me.

"I have a list of names for you to choose from," Mordecai continued. "I'll bring them home tonight so you can help us make a choice. Meanwhile, I think you should learn some things about what it is like to live at court."

A sudden knock at the door brought them both to their feet, and the look in Mordecai's eyes told Hadassah he was expecting someone. When Hadassah opened the door, she saw a well-dressed man standing there on the doorstep.

"Glad to see you," Mordecai said, extending a hand to the stranger. "This is Zarbanu, a royal chamberlain from the palace," Mordecai glanced at Hadassah. "He's here to instruct you on the rules of etiquette in the palace. He can tell you what you should wear, what you can expect to eat, and how you should behave. He also has advice on what kinds of things you should say when you are spoken to and what you cannot afford to say."

Esther was stunned but said nothing. What could she say? Everything Mordecai had said would happen was unfolding before her very eyes—and it frightened her.

Zarbanu spent two days teaching Hadassah everything he knew about life in the royal palace. By the time he left at the end of the second day, she was much more at ease about what it might be like to have to live in the court of the king. They had discussed everything from foods to clothing to the conversations she could expect to have with members of the royal family.

By now everyone in the Jewish community was sure the inevitable would happen. Hadassah would likely be summoned to the palace to join the beauty competition. The king's courtiers would find her in the marketplace or at the public cistern, or they would come knocking at her door. There was no way they would miss her. She was too stunningly attractive, perfect in every way for a contest of this sort. She would be exactly what they were looking for.

A few days later, during the morning meal, there was a knock at the door once again. Hadassah glanced at Mordecai and Aunt Bithiah, her eyes growing wide. Goose bumps ran up and down her arms, as she sensed that something big was about to happen. And she was right. Two courtiers from the palace had arrived with a summons for Hadassah. She was to report immediately to Ardalan at the royal palace, where all the candidates of the beauty competition were gathering.

Hadassah was calm and collected on the outside, but inside she was panicking. Time was up! Everything was happening so fast! She began to think of everything that could go wrong! What if she forgot her manners or said all the wrong things or ate all the wrong foods? What if she didn't make it into the final rounds of the competition? Worse yet, what if she did?

She looked to Mordecai for assurance, but he only nodded in the direction of the two courtiers. "Go with the men," he urged quietly. "You can send for your personal things later."

A slow drizzle was coming down as Hadassah followed the two representatives through the brick paved streets. The month of Kislev had brought its usual rains. *What a day for the court officials to come for me!* Hadassah thought. She pulled her warm cloak close around her to calm her shivering body. Suddenly she felt very frightened and very much alone.

But there was no time to be feeling sorry for herself. Her big day had arrived, and whether she liked it or not, she was being summoned as one of the potential candidates in the king's beauty competition.

It soon became obvious that they were headed in the direction of the royal citadel and the palace grounds surrounding it. Palm

trees and exotic plants lined the streets and walkways leading toward the palace complex. Buildings made of sun-baked bricks
stood straight and tall, rising to the rain-soaked sky. Across their
blue-bricked walls were murals of lions, bulls, and dragons.

Hadassah tried not to look wide-eyed as she and the court representatives entered an impressive-looking building through
vaulted doorways. This place was grand beyond anything she had
ever dreamed of in her wildest imagination. She had heard Cousin
Mordecai describe the extravagant accommodations of the royal
court, but she didn't remember him mentioning these kinds of
details.

CHAPTER 11

Hadassah had never been inside a palace of any kind, let alone the palace complex of the most powerful king in the world. What she saw now was truly astonishing! High ceilings, arching doorways, and expansive widows with ornate dressings of purple, blue, and white were set deep in the palace walls. Exotic potted plants of every size and sort decorated the rooms. Couches covered with red and blue cushions occupied the corners, while rugs and floor cushions filled the floor space in front of them.

Inside the palace complex, charcoal burners here and there took the chill out of the air. Because the day was gray and cloudy, lamps had been lit.

But the thing that surprised Hadassah the most was the number of other young maidens who had arrived there before her. There were scores of them, tall and short, with black, deep brown, and even auburn hair—but it was obvious they had all been chosen for their beauty. The young women milled around on the white marble floor of the great hall until an important-looking court official came in and made an announcement.

"Form a line over here, girls." He pointed toward a large doorway that led to another room. "We'll begin the interviews now."

Hadassah moved into line behind a tall brunette. She was glad she wasn't first in line. This way she would know what to say and do. Right now she was nervous and didn't want to say anything to anyone. She didn't know any of the other girls, and she wasn't sure whether talking was allowed. Anyway, no one else was talking. She studied the faces of the other girls, but tried not to be obvious about it. Some looked confident, some a bit proud, but most simply looked anxious.

Then she noticed the court official. The man was wearing a green robe of fine linen, and a broad crimson belt encircled his waist. His hair was jet-black and braided in the back, and his beard was braided too. Hadassah wondered if this was the Ardalan she was supposed to report to, but he hadn't introduced himself.

"Your name?" the official asked the first girl in line.

The dark-haired girl bowed her head, her eyes on the floor. "Sudoova," she said quietly.

"Please step this way." The official pointed through the doorway, and with that the two of them disappeared out of sight.

The line moved slowly but steadily all morning, but just before noon when it was almost Hadassah's turn, a court attendant announced they would begin the noon rest period. That meant Hadassah would have to wait some more. It made her tired just thinking about standing in line all that time. She wished she could just go home. She wished she could go back to her room in the house of Mordecai in the Jewish community. But she knew that wasn't an option. By royal decree she couldn't go anywhere until she had been reviewed by whoever it was that was interviewing the maidens.

"Please be seated in the wing to the right of the receiving room." The court official pointed to yet another expansive chamber and smiled. "Give your feet a rest, and we'll serve you some refreshments in a few moments."

They all sat down on the deep floor cushions scattered across the large carpets, while servants served them delightful things to eat. A parade of waiters brought silver platters decorated with greenery and exotic flowers and loaded with the finest finger foods the palace cooks had to offer. The food looked delicious. There were crackers, small biscuit-shaped breads, slices of fruit, and plenty of spreads and cheeses. Hadassah's mouth watered as she realized that the anxiety of waiting all morning had made her ravenous with hunger.

But much of what she saw on the silver trays smelled strange. There were lots and lots of meats, and many of them were kinds Hadassah had never seen before. Some were little cuts of red meat; others were diced into tiny cubes for easy dipping with the crackers. But the meats that made Hadassah the most suspicious were the ones with little black eyes. Whatever those little creatures were, it was obvious they weren't kosher for a Jewish girl to eat. She tried not to stare at them as they looked up at her from their little beds of green herbs.

"No, thank you," Hadassah had to say over and over again to the delicacies being offered her. She knew she would never violate the Jewish vows she had taken for eating only kosher food and beverages. She did eat a few of the breads with cheeses. Then she spied some olives and melon slices and took several samples from that tray. Finally, a waiter brought in some figs and grapes, and soon she was feeling more relaxed.

But the wait was longer than Hadassah had expected. Evidently, the government officials were enjoying their noon break too. No doubt some were probably even taking a little nap. Just as Hadassah was becoming drowsy and thinking she might catch a little nap where she sat on her cushion, the distinguished-looking official returned.

A court crier loudly announced, "Ardalan will now commence with the remaining interviews!"

"So this is Ardalan, after all," Hadassah mumbled to herself, and then suddenly the official was announcing her name. "Esther of Susa!" he called out, using the Persian name she had given the scribe when she first arrived at the receiving room.

CHAPTER 12

Hadassah stepped forward, bowing her head to stare at the floor as was the custom for any maiden, even in a beauty contest. She knew she needed to think of herself as Esther and not as Hadassah from now on. It would be the safest thing to do if she had to stay in the palace for a while.

"You were registered here in Susa." Ardalan glanced at Esther's name on the list of names inscribed on a scroll in his hand. "Where is your home of origin?" he continued, not bothering to glance up at Esther.

"The city of Addan." Esther watched the official's eyes, and then quickly added, "My parents died, and I came to Susa to live with relatives."

Ardalan said something to the recording scribe, and then finally turned to look at her. "Can you read Persian well enough to—" but he never finished his sentence. He just stared at her, opened his mouth several times to say something, but stopped as though at a loss for words. Finally, he did manage a weak, "Oh my!" and then began scrutinizing her from the crown of her raven head to the soles of her feet.

He stepped toward her and lifted her chin to look at her face and neck. "You have strong but gentle lines," he said. "Regal. Very regal indeed." The man turned to speak with one of the officials standing nearby, but Esther couldn't hear everything he was saying. She did catch snatches of the conversation, though. "Stunning eyes . . . clear skin . . . mature . . . respectful . . . very appealing." It was obvious Ardalan and the other official were impressed with her. They certainly were taking more time with her than they had with many of the other young maidens.

Finally, they smiled at her and motioned for her to follow them through the doorways of the great hall. They took a wide corridor under a portico and passed through a garden before entering another building, this one more lavish than the first one.

Guards dressed in the best of royal attire stood as sentinels at every doorway. Their heads were covered with the colorful mitered helmets, their faces stern and expressionless.

When Ardalan opened a set of interior doors, Esther caught her breath. The room was constructed with red marble floors and high ceilings decorated in designs of gold overleaf. Golden lamps on the walls burned scented oils, reflecting their lights in mirrors everywhere. As she walked with the two officials from room to room, beautiful young maidens stared at Esther, their expressions of jealous suspicion too obvious to hide.

As Esther watched their reactions to her arrival, she was sure this must be a group of finalists already separated from the rest of the contestants.

"Good afternoon, girls," Ardalan greeted them. "This is Esther, our most recent finalist in the contest." Esther was met with a few polite smiles, but more cool stares.

Ardalan took Esther on a small tour of the rest of the girls' quarters and then finally opened double doors to an expansive apartment. A room with a high ceiling and broad window opened on a garden outside. "These will be your chambers here," he said, bowing his head with respect for this amazing girl who had completely captured everyone's attention by now.

Ardalan left Esther standing in the doorway to the apartment and turned to the fifteen or twenty young girls lounging in the receiving room. "See that Esther feels welcome." Several girls scowled at this remark, but Ardalan held up his hand as if to silence the troublemakers among them.

He nodded toward two chamberlains who stepped from a side room. "Where's Hegai?" Ardalan asked. "Will he be back soon?"

One of the attendants shook his head. "He's gone to the royal harem to speak with Shaashgaz. He should be back after the evening meal."

"All right then, I have to be going now, but I'll be in from time to time to see how the new finalist is doing." He glanced toward Esther's suite of rooms and then toward the group of girls and raised his eyebrows. "Let me know if Esther needs anything," he told them. "Anything at all."

After Ardalan left, Esther walked to the window to stare out on the garden walkways lined with flowering plants and palms. Spouting fountains and statues of gods and goddesses filled every little nook. Colorful birds sang from the branches of the greenery. A light rain had begun to fall again, so Esther pulled the window shutters closed and turned to survey her room.

A bed sat in the very center of the room, with a large vanity to one side. Small couches and tables filled the other corners of the room, and there were mirrors and green potted plants everywhere. Little yellow birds sang from a cage near the window, and a low table with a tray of sweets sat ready for her to taste, should she so desire.

Esther sat down to rest on a red couch. "What a place!" she gasped. "How can this have happened to me? Am I dreaming?"

And where is Cousin Mordecai? she wondered. *Does he miss me? Are he and Aunt Bithiah worried about me?* She wished they were here with her now. It seemed so long ago that she had left home, but she knew it had been only that morning.

Esther walked over to the bed and lay down on its gold-embroidered covering. By now her head was swimming with thoughts of everything that had happened to her in just one short day. In all her daydreams, she had never thought about becoming part of a beauty contest! Her wildest imagining could not grasp the possibility of being chosen as queen.

Just that morning she had been called to the palace as a beauty contestant. The court officials had been surprised and delighted with her stunning looks and personality. Evidently, they had already chosen to promote her as a finalist and had taken her to live in the quarters where the finalists were staying. They had given her a fine suite of rooms, and she wondered if that meant there was a chance she might become a wife of the king. That was what Cousin Mordecai had said might happen should she make it this far.

Esther didn't even want to think about what it would be like to become King Xerxes' queen, but she did stop to think about how all this might fit into God's plan for her life.

And then she dozed. How long she slept she didn't know, but when a knock sounded at the door, she quickly sat up.

CHAPTER 13

"May I come in?" A young woman about Esther's age poked her head around the doorway. "Am I disturbing you?"

Esther smoothed her hair down self-consciously and rubbed the sleep from her eyes. "Yes! I mean no, that's fine! Please do come in." She swung her feet over the side of the bed and went to greet the girl at the door.

The girl was beautiful to look at, with long auburn hair. Her eyelashes were unusually long, and the eyes behind them were an unusual shade of amber that matched her hair perfectly.

"Peace be to you," she said. "My name is Droxshana, but you can call me Shan if you like." She gazed at Esther sweetly.

"Thank you. Peace be to you," was all Esther could say.

"It's almost time for the evening meal." Droxshana opened the shutters and looked at the beautiful garden. The sun had finally come out, but was near the horizon. "Would you like to go with me?"

"Yes," Esther hesitated only a moment. "That would be very nice. I don't know anyone here, and this is all—so—intimidating." She tried not to use big words and sound sophisticated, but intimidated was exactly how she felt. Even while Hadassah was very young, Mordecai and Bithiah had always talked to her as though she were an adult, and now it made her sound like the classy, educated young maiden she appeared to be. The average girl of her day couldn't read or write, let alone carry on a cultured conversation, so Esther knew she was going to have to watch herself. The last thing she wanted was to have people think that she put on airs and tried to act superior to the other girls.

At the evening meal, the girls all knelt around large circular tables. The meal was sumptuous. It wasn't supposed to be a banquet, but it might as well have been. There were all kinds of delicacies for the girls to choose from—fruit cups and little crackers and cheese spreads. And there were many foods Esther didn't recognize. A fermented fishy smell wafted up from some of trays of delicacies. She was sure they were creatures from the sea and definitely off-limits for a Jew. Any seafood was forbidden unless it had scales.

Because this was a ladies' meal, it included none of the food that a men's meal might feature, such as snake meat, large insects, and even mice. The thought of such things made Esther's skin crawl. Jews were permitted to eat grasshoppers and crickets, but just about anything else that crept along on the ground was an abomination to the Lord.

Esther watched everything Droxshana did at the meal. She knew she couldn't afford any blunders. And then she remembered the advice Zarbanu had given her while tutoring her in court etiquette. For two intensive days, he had tried to prepare her to blend in well with palace society.

The other girls in the banquet room were watching her. She could tell by the silence that settled over the room when she and Droxshana had entered, but again she tried to ignore their cold looks and haughty stares. This was going to be a difficult time for her just as Zarbanu had warned. To greet them all seemed like the right thing to do, but she left this up to Droxshana.

When the meal had ended and they had stayed for what seemed to be the right amount of time, Droxshana nodded at all the girls. "Peace be to you all," she offered politely, but only one or two of the girls returned her greeting.

As she and Esther stood to leave, an uncomfortable murmur rippled through the room, but Droxshana shrugged them off as she took Esther by the arm. "Come," she whispered, looking over her shoulder, "let's go somewhere private so we can talk."

Droxshana led Esther out of the room and settled them on a couch covered with a fabric of gold and turquoise. When the two had made themselves comfortable, Droxshana lowered her voice. "The others are just jealous."

"Jealous?" Esther blinked, her eyes big with surprise. "Why would they be jealous?"

"You're joking." Droxshana gave a little laugh that sounded like a rippling brook. "Just look at you! You're gorgeous! I haven't seen anyone in here with your status!"

"Me?" Esther could hardly believe Droxshana was talking about her. "Why me? The others are just as beautiful as I am." She continued staring at Droxshana. "And what about you? Your hair is the most beautiful auburn I've ever seen. And your eyes . . ." Esther's voice trailed off.

"Beautiful, yes, but stunning? That's not me or the others. You've got something different from the rest of us. What is it?"

Esther blinked again, staring at Droxshana. "What is what? I haven't the slightest notion what you're talking about." And it was true. She was naive, and anyone looking on would have said so, but Esther herself had no idea to what extent.

Droxshana shook her head unbelievingly. "This is incredible! Here you are, one of the most beautiful girls I've ever seen, and you're completely unaware of it! Amazing!" she kept saying. "Truly amazing!"

CHAPTER 14

The sun had finally set, its golden rays turning to amber and then pink and rose. The evening birds had already begun their night songs, and everywhere the cool of the evening was coming on. Esther felt as if she were in a dream. What could she expect next?

That evening Ardalan came by to see how the girls were doing. When he entered the room, the girls all arose and stood respectfully. With him was another distinguished-looking man, one Esther hadn't yet met. Esther could tell his status by the golden fringe on the hem of his ruby-red tunic. "This is Hegai, the officer in charge of the young maidens in the contest."

Ardalan's eyes surveyed the group of girls, and then he spied Esther. "And this is the one I was telling you about," he said, as he made his way to where she was standing. He reached out, took her hand, and drew Esther toward him. "Meet Esther," he said, bowing to her politely as though she were some kind of royalty. "Truly a remarkable girl!"

But it was obvious that Hegai had already noticed Esther, and the look in his eyes was one of pure wonder. "Yes, I can see that!" he murmured. "I can see that." He would have been embarrassed to know that his mouth had dropped open at the sight of her, but it was the truth. It was as if he had forgotten his place as an important dignitary in the royal citadel of Susa. But he didn't care.

Several days passed, and Esther kept to herself. There was

nothing else it seemed she could do about the cool stares being sent her way. The girls were silent toward her when they ate their meals together. They gave Esther the cold shoulder whenever they saw her coming from her suite of rooms. Something was clearly wrong, but she didn't know what it could be. It was as though the girls had all agreed to shun her. It was as though someone or something was engineering this whole thing to make Esther feel all alone.

Droxshana tried to make her feel at home, and if it hadn't been for her friendship, Esther would have been totally miserable. Oh how she missed Cousin Mordecai and Aunt Bithiah. She was beginning to wish very much that she had never come to the palace at all. Not that she had any choice in the matter.

One evening, things really got out of hand. One would have thought that by now the other maidens would be showing Esther some respect since she had been so well received by Ardalan and Hegai. Unfortunately, the opposite was proving to be true.

"Well now!" one of the raven-haired damsels sneered when Esther and Droxshana entered the dining hall. "If it isn't the beauty queen herself, come to dine among the likes of us!" The girl's coal-black eyes flashed angrily as she stepped in front of Esther and glared at her. "You're nobody, girl! Do you understand? Nobody! I know all about you!"

"Mind your own business, Manija!" Droxshana tried to come to Esther's rescue, but it was no use.

Manija's eyes flashed at Esther. "You're an orphan, from a family of no importance! No royal blood flows in your veins! You're an impostor, a poor girl, and when Hegai finds out, he'll have you sent down so fast, you'll be dizzy!"

Esther stared at Manija silently. She didn't know what to say. What could she say? Everything Manija said was true except that she wasn't an impostor. The only thing Manija hadn't said was that Esther was a Jew, and Cousin Mordecai had urged her to keep that a secret. Now she could see the wisdom behind such a warning. There was no telling what a person like Manija could do with that bit of information.

"Leave her alone!" Droxshana almost shouted this time. "What's she done to you?"

But Manija wasn't listening. She began another tirade again, this time swearing at Esther as if the girl was her worst enemy. Manija was so loud, in fact, and so caught up in her attack that she never noticed when two court officials entered the room.

But the fear on all the other girls' faces finally caught her attention. She whirled around to face Hegai and Shaashgaz, who frowned at her sternly.

"That will be quite enough!" Hegai snapped. He glanced at his fellow officer, Shaashgaz, chief official in charge of the king's harem. Almost instantly, Manija became the demure, quiet girl she wanted the officials to see, but it was too late.

"Guards! Throw this young woman out of the palace!" Hegai snapped. "Send her back to her family! I won't have her staying here even one more night!" Two stern palace guards rushed to do his bidding.

"Please!" Manija begged, falling to her knees on the red marble floor. "I beg your forgiveness. I've made a serious mistake and wish to make it right!"

But Hegai would have none of it. "You are quite correct about that!" he replied. "You have made a serious mistake! As to how you can make up for the blunder? Leave at once before I have you flogged!"

CHAPTER 15

Esther was astonished at this turn of events! Just a few minutes before, she herself had been a victim of ridicule, but now, even in this pagan palace, justice was being served. Esther was being treated fairly, and so was Manija.

The guards led Manija from the room, crying as if she were being led away to prison. And in some ways, she was. For the rest of her days, she would live in shame. After being considered as a candidate for the king's royal harem and possibly even the position of queen, she was being thrown out as though she were trash.

"And now, young lady," Hegai was looking straight at Esther, "I would like you to get your personal things together and come with us."

Esther opened her mouth, but then closed it again. She didn't know what to say, but decided whatever she could possibly say would be better left unsaid for now anyway. Where they were taking her was again a mystery, but if it had something to do with Manija's outbursts, she was better off being silent.

She felt exhilarated and yet alone as they marched off through more corridors. The cool of the evening greeted them as they passed through lush gardens of greenery and flowering shrubs, and then back again through palace porticos. Now and then the night sounds of Susa could be heard wafting up and over the palace walls. The faint cries of a baby, the barking of a dog—each reminded her of the people she had left behind. Common people with ordinary lives and ordinary dreams.

Guards flanked them as Esther and the two officers made their way along dimly lit walkways. From time to time, an unfortunate moth would flutter up against one of the torches only to fall lifeless to the ground. In some ways, Esther felt helpless like that moth. She had no choice in where she was going, no choice about where the turns of her life would lead. Only God could understand, and again, she turned everything over to Him. With Him she felt safe and secure. With Him she didn't need to worry about what was coming next.

They walked on for some time, finally coming to a large, imposing iron gate. Hegai shouted some instructions, and when the gate finally creaked open, they entered a patio with a floor of mosaics surrounded by another luxurious garden. A few lamps lit the way, but even in the darkness, Esther could see that the garden was filled with more exotic plants and flowers, no doubt a sight to behold during daylight hours.

More commands were shouted, and then several more gates opened before they finally entered a palace suite that was truly spectacular! Again Esther was overwhelmed by the extravagance of the place. Again intricately designed gold overlay was everywhere, and black obsidian floors were polished to a fine sheen. This was obviously an important place in the royal complex, but Esther had no idea where.

Hegai clapped his hands, and immediately two royal chamberlains appeared. They bowed from the waist, their hands together as a symbol of submission.

"Gentlemen, this is Esther, our newest addition to the royal harem. See that she gets the best treatment." Hegai smiled at Esther. "In fact, why don't you get her settled in the royal Simona

Suite," he directed. The chamberlains glanced at one another and then bowed to Hegai again. "Yes, master," was their reply.

"You'll be better off here," Hegai assured Esther, noting her wide eyes. "I wasn't going to move you to the harem this soon, but after I saw the treatment you were receiving tonight, I decided to move things forward a bit more quickly. I can't have a woman of your caliber being treated in this manner."

He frowned. "If I wasn't so kind, Manija's fate would have been worse, but," and he sighed, "all of that is behind us now. I trust that you will be more comfortable here. Is there anything at all you desire before I go?" he glanced toward the waiting chamberlains. "Bemun and Feloma will be here to tend to your every need."

Hegai waited as though actually expecting Esther to make a request. She could tell by the expression on his face that she could probably have anything she wanted, but honestly, he had done enough for her already. What else did she need?

"Well . . . there is one thing," she finally asked, hesitating, "if it's not too much trouble, would it be possible for Droxshana to come visit me now and then? I don't know anyone in the palace, and she's been such a good friend to me."

"I think I can arrange that." Hegai winked at Esther. "Now get some rest, young lady. I'll be by tomorrow about midmorning. We've got a lot to do."

And with that he was gone, leaving Esther with the chamberlains. As was the custom, they were to be in charge of her suite of rooms, her meals, and any communications she might want to have with the rest of the palace. She wondered how she would ever get used to this kind of arrangement, but she knew she had no choice.

Bemun opened the double doors to her suite and stepped back to allow her to pass into the extravagant chambers beyond. The apartment was enormous, with a high ceiling and windows overlooking the darkened gardens beyond. Couches covered with satin and silk were placed in attractive locations around the room, and on them were cushions with gold and silver embroidery. Small tables of ebony sat on each end of the couches, with vases of flowers on them and small trays of bite-sized snacks.

"Will you be needing anything else before we retire for the night?" Bemun asked, his head bowed respectfully.

"Um . . . no!" Esther blushed. "Everything's wonderful."

He backed his way out of the room, leaving Esther to explore her new quarters. A large sandalwood table for dining nearly filled another room of the suite. And through another doorway was a room with what appeared to be a bathtub sunken into the marble-tiled floor. But it was much bigger than a tub—in fact, more like a small swimming pool.

The suite was luxurious beyond her wildest expectations. After only a few days in the palace, she had already been elevated to the status of competition finalist and perhaps even a potential wife in the royal harem! For a girl just sixteen years of age, that seemed too good to be true—or too frightening to fathom—one or the other, and she wasn't exactly sure which. Truly, truly, she was being blessed beyond anything she could have possibly dreamed.

CHAPTER 16

The next morning, Hegai returned as promised. "Let me introduce you to the others in the king's harem," he said, standing in the doorway to Esther's suite. When he saw a look of anxiety cross Esther's face, he smiled. "I know what you're thinking! You're worried that the king's wives in the harem won't accept you because you're young and beautiful. Am I right?"

Esther blushed, but Hegai smiled and patted her slender shoulder. "I don't think it will be quite the same in this case as it was with the beauty contestants. There may be one or two of the wives who feel threatened by you, but for the most part, they'll welcome you, I think."

"But if I'm a candidate for queen, won't that cause the wives to resent me?"

"For a while, perhaps, but one thing's for sure, if by chance you did become a serious contender for the position of queen, most of the wives would probably want to work their way into your good graces. It would be in their best interest to do that, don't you think?"

Hegai smiled again at Esther. "After what happened to Queen Vashti three years ago, everyone is still waiting to see what will happen next. But everything will be OK," he added gently, watching Esther's expression. "You'll see."

Esther seemed to relax a bit at these comments, but inside she still worried. *Can I believe Hegai? Can I trust him?* She was afraid to trust anyone completely right now, but she was afraid to depend on her own instincts too. How could she know who might be a friend in this pagan palace? How could she know who might be an enemy in disguise? If one of the wives should find out she was a Jewess, would it make a difference? On the other hand, would anyone even care?

She glanced at Hegai. "What actually did happen to Vashti? I've heard a lot about her, but you never can tell how much of what you hear is true."

"That's right." Hegai nodded. "Stories do seem to expand every time they're told. But Vashti? Well, now, she was a classy lady. Everything good they've said about her is true. On the night she was thrown out of the harem and lost her place as queen, the king was having one of his famous parties. All the lords and officers of his realm were with him in the royal banquet hall—governors, satraps, ambassadors, military generals. This particular party was just one of many in a grand six-month celebration designed to impress these important officers in his kingdom. He was planning a war with Greece in the west and wanted their support.

"The celebration was extravagant—parties every night, sports events, dancing contests for all his wives—but the party on this night was the worst one of all. By midnight the king and all the lords were drunk. They were so drunk, in fact, that by now no one was making sense anymore. They were all singing and laughing and carrying on in despicable ways." Hegai leaned out the open doorway of Esther's suite to see if there might be anyone listening in on their conversation.

"So anyway, as they were watching the women dancing, one of the king's generals suggested they might like to see Vashti dance. So the king sent Mehuman and his other chamberlains down here to the harem to bring Queen Vashti up to the feast. I wasn't the head chamberlain for the queen, but Shaashgaz was out for the moment, and we couldn't locate him, so I was the next man in charge.

" 'The king wants to see the queen dance,' the king's head chamberlain said rudely, without so much as a thought as to how Queen Vashti might feel about it."

Hegai rolled his eyes. "Now I knew the queen had been entertaining the wives of all the dignitaries that had come to Susa for King Xerxes' celebrations. But it was late, and I wasn't sure the queen would even be up. When we went to the queen's private banquet hall in the citadel, sure enough, the place was empty except for a few servants cleaning up. They told us Queen Vashti had taken a few of her closest friends back to her royal suite.

"Anyway, when we arrived at the doors of her private chambers, I was wondering what I would say to this elegant lady. I didn't think Vashti was going to take kindly to having the king drag her out in front of all those drunken lords, and I was sure she wouldn't want to dance for them like some foolish belly dancer." Hegai frowned and shook his head in disgust. "But you don't tell the most powerful man in the world something like that!" He sighed. "You just don't. I hesitated at her door, but not for long. Only long enough to give Mehuman a chance to think about what he was asking me to do."

Hegai hung his head at the memory. "It didn't make any difference. Mehuman said the king was drunker than drunk, and if we didn't do something quickly, he might end up a raving lunatic. By now I realized I had to do this. Nothing was going to stop the king in his demand to make the queen parade herself around in front of everybody.

"And, of course, when the door to the queen's suite finally opened and we told Shirin, her head chamberlain, about the king's demand, he looked really worried too."

Esther watched Hegai's eyes. He was reliving the story as if it had all happened just yesterday.

This was the first time she had heard the tale in all its detail, and what better person to tell it than Hegai himself. After all, he was an eyewitness. Esther didn't say anything, but her eyebrows were asking a hundred questions all at once.

"Of course, she refused to go, just as I thought she would," Hegai continued the story with pride. "We all knew there would be a price to pay for it, but we cheered for her anyway. Of course, we had no idea how much it would cost us. We all loved Queen Vashti. I don't know anyone who didn't like her. As I've said, she was a first-class lady. The best!"

Hegai hung his head. "I don't know why I'm telling you all of this. I guess I feel as though I can trust you. The gods know I can't trust anyone around here anymore with the king's informers everywhere. But you? You're different, Esther. You're so uncomplicated and down-to-earth. You're so honest in appearance, and— and it seems a secret told you in confidence would die with you before you would betray the friend who had shared it."

The man was indeed opening himself up to her, and Esther was surprised. After all, he was a court official, a man of importance in the palace complex. She was only a girl, and a young one at that.

Hegai blinked as if he, too, realized what was happening. There was something very appealing about the innocence and simplicity of this beautiful girl, and he felt the warmth of an unseen presence when he was around her. He could not know it was the Spirit of God attending Esther everywhere she went. But he sensed it.

He shook himself as if to come back to the reality of the moment and then glanced cautiously into the empty receiving room once more before continuing with the tale. He knew he needed to be careful when he talked like this, even if it was just to Esther. You could never tell if someone else might be listening.

CHAPTER 17

Hegai grinned sheepishly. "You know the rest of the story," he said, lowering his voice. "The king threw Queen Vashti out. At the advice of his closest counselors, he sent her packing! Left her with nothing but the clothes in her wardrobe and the estate he had given her in Persepolis, another royal city in the Persian Empire."

Hegai studied Esther's expression. "So you see, it's not easy being queen, but if anyone could do it, I'm guessing you could. And if you should be so fortunate, I for one would welcome you as the new queen. You would certainly bring a breath of fresh air to the citadel." He smiled again. "And who knows, you might find yourself making more friends around here than you expected."

"More friends than I expected? That doesn't sound very encouraging." Esther looked frightened again and dared to look Hegai in the eye. "I wish someone had told me the whole story about Vashti before I came to the palace." She lowered her eyes again. "It might have changed things a bit for me."

Hegai began to laugh softly. "Hmm, I doubt it. Like all the other maidens in the realm, if you were beautiful, you had no choice about showing up for the royal interview."

"I know, I know—but, at least if I had known all this, I could have done things a little differently."

"Like?" Hegai raised his eyebrows.

"Like disguise myself by rubbing a heavy dose of mud or charcoal on my face every morning before I went to the marketplace or the public cistern to get water. Maybe then I wouldn't have been so appealing!"

"Very funny! Very funny!" Hegai shook his head at Esther. "I can see you're going to be a pleasant young woman to have around the palace. I've never met a finer lady than you. And so young. How old did you say you are?"

"Sixteen."

Hegai whistled. "Sixteen! So young, and yet so beautiful. So poised and full of life. I can only imagine what the king will say when he finally gets to see you!"

"When will that be?"

"Not for a year," he smiled, "but don't worry, we've got lots to do before then."

"A whole year?" Esther's eyes grew excited again. Her voice sounded surprised, but the look on her face was one of relief.

"Twelve months—six months for oil of myrrh and other lotions and ointments to soften your complexion, and six more months so we can sweeten you up with perfumes and cosmetics." Hegai rolled his eyes again. "Not that you need any sweetening.

"After that you'll be taken to the king for his own personal inspection. You and all the other finalists who've already entered the second level of the contest. Selecting you out of the two thousand contestants was the biggest job, but now that that part is nearly over, it's going to be a bit easier. All we have to do now is prepare the girls we've chosen so they can meet the king. Then, of course, he'll make the final choice. I must say I was worried at the start about whether we were going to be able to find someone who could measure up to his expectations, but—well, now I'm not so worried anymore." He winked at Esther, but she missed the look completely.

"So you must have found lots of beautiful young women who qualify?"

Hegai shook his head. "No, Esther, I don't think you understand. Finding beautiful women is not the problem. Finding one who can fill the shoes of Queen Vashti—I mean the former Queen Vashti—that's the trouble."

"She was that good?"

"She was more than good. She was stunning! She was regal! Poised, proper, and always elegant. There will never be another Vashti."

"Hmm, I can see you do have your work cut out for you." Esther rolled her eyes too. "I don't envy you, Hegai." She bowed her head in respect to this man who had such an important, and yet precarious job in the palace. Manager of the king's royal harem? Esther was sure Hegai had a job that would never be ordinary!

"Now, let's get you something to eat." Hegai clapped his hands. "Then we'll introduce you to some of the ladies-in-waiting." Within moments, Bemun, the chamberlain, arrived with a large tray of foods from which she could choose.

"I hope what we have here this morning is good enough for you," Hegai apologized. "You're going to have to tell us exactly what you like to eat. Every young lady here in the palace is different. We'll soon learn what you do and don't like, but until then, you're going to have to be patient with us." He stepped through the doorway and then turned again as an afterthought. "Oh, there is one more thing, and I apologize for not telling you sooner, Esther. You'll be assigned seven young maidens to attend you. I'll send them over before noon."

Esther looked surprised again. "But Bemun and Feloma? What about them?"

"Oh, they're just your chamberlains. They don't stay in your quarters. They're your servants to do all the real work around here. Things like bringing your meals, getting your clothes ready each time you need to go out, running messages to the rest of the palace complex."

"And the maidens?"

Hegai smiled at the beautiful girl standing before him. "Your maidens will live here in the servants' quarters. They'll be helping you with all your beauty treatments and dress you and go with you whenever you leave the harem complex here at the citadel."

Esther's eyes brightened with excitement. "I'm going to get to leave the palace grounds sometimes?" The thought of being cooped up in the harem complex, though it was luxurious, was depressing to her. She wasn't used to the restrictions on her freedom, but she also realized she was just going to have to get used to it. Her life had changed so much since she had been brought into the palace for the beauty contest. Things would never be the same again! *Never!*

"Thank you so much for all you've done to make me feel welcome!" Esther smiled sweetly at Hegai, grateful that God had given her someone almost as kind as Mordecai himself.

After Esther ate a light morning meal of figs, melon, and yogurt flavored with a few sweetened berries, Hegai made sure she was dressed in the finest garment of her wardrobe. A robe of blue silk with a golden sash seemed to be just the outfit to make the right impression in her introduction to the others in the harem. Then he took her out among the wives who had already gathered in the receiving room where it was customary for guests to be greeted and entertained.

"Ladies." Hegai paused and bowed. "I'd like to introduce you to Esther, a recent arrival in the royal beauty contest. We found her right here in Susa. Can you imagine that!"

A wave of smiles traveled through the group of women. Esther counted eighteen of them. She didn't know how many wives there were in the entire harem, but these looked harmless enough. Time would tell, of course.

One thing was sure, though. She knew she was going to have to get used to her new name. Though she was a Jewess, she needed to look like a Persian woman, act like a Persian woman, and even think like a Persian woman.

CHAPTER 18

Seven young maidens-in-waiting came to live with Esther in the harem complex as Hegai had promised. There was Morvari, a tall, slim girl with long, dark hair, and Ovoga, who had deep, dark eyes. Two of the girls were sisters, Kahin and Keshvar, recently captured in an uprising in the city of Babylon. Taamina was short and petite, with a vivacious, lively personality. Parvona was the quiet one, with gentle hands and a kind face. And Mahin. Esther thought she and Mahin probably had more in common than the others. Mahin was very religious, and althought quite beautiful, she kept to herself. All the girls were young, none of them older than twenty. Their one purpose in life now was to help prepare Esther for the final phase of the beauty contest.

And so the routine began. Esther awoke every morning to a light breakfast served up by Bemun, her chamberlain. On warm, sunny mornings, she sat in the harem courtyard, taking her meal while exotic birds serenaded her with their bright, cheerful songs. On cool mornings, she sat by an open fire burning in a charcoal burner.

Then at midmorning came the beauty ritual of oils and lotions that Hegai had instructed Esther's attending maidens to give her. Kahin and Keshvar were in charge of the skin treatments with ointments and lotions. Every morning, they pounded fragrant herbs and resins into a creamy paste using a mortar and pestle.

Myrrh and roshoor were two of the most common ingredients ideal for softening the skin. Using sesame and olive oils, Morvari prepared the fragrant oils Esther would need, and Parvona was the expert responsible for Esther's hair. The rest of the girls laid out Esther's clothes each day and saw to the hundred and one other needs she might have. It was wonderful being pampered like this, and to Esther, it all seemed too good to be true.

One day when Esther was standing at her window, she saw a familiar figure pacing back and forth just beyond the main gate to the harem palace. It was Cousin Mordecai. He seemed to be anxious about something and kept looking through the metal bars of the gate. She hadn't seen him for several weeks now and had wanted to get in touch with him, but hadn't thought of a good way to do it. Esther knew she had to be careful. She didn't know any of her attending maidens very well, and Hegai seemed kind—but could she trust him? As of yet, no one knew that Mordecai was her cousin, so the secret of her identity as a Jew was still safe. Mordecai had warned her to be very careful with that information in the palace, and that was exactly what she intended to do.

But now when she saw Mordecai at the gate, she seemed to lose some of the caution that had kept her so careful up to now. Esther waved at him excitedly and finally got his attention. For several long moments, they stared at one another, and then he smiled and turned away. Suddenly, an idea came to her. She called her chamberlain and asked for parchment and a writing quill. She would send messages to the royal archives where he worked, asking him to send her copies of scrolls with literature and history just like he used to do when she was living at home. After all, Hegai had told her that was one of the jobs of the chamberlains.

Immediately, she wrote a letter to Mordecai telling him everything that had happened to her. She told him about her first day with the other young maidens in the palace and about the interviews with the king's officers. She told him about being moved to the special apartment that first day and about Droxshana's friendship. She shared the incident with Manija and how the girl had been dismissed from the contest because of the way she had treated Esther.

Esther had so much to tell Mordecai that she couldn't stop writing. She told Mordecai about Hegai, the director of the harem, about how he had moved her a second time to better quarters because of the way she was being treated. She told him of the seven maidens assigned to attend her every need and that she was getting accustomed to her Persian name.

The chamberlain delivered the message to Mordecai, but it wasn't until two days later that he brought back a reply. Esther wondered why Mordecai had taken so long to get a message back to her, but she knew he probably had a good reason. He was a busy man. And then again, when she really thought about it, she guessed he would want to be careful about sending messages to her. As he had said before, he would want to be careful not to give away her identity.

And as things worked out, from then on, Esther used this method to communicate with Mordecai. It worked perfectly. Whenever she wanted to get a message to Mordecai, she would send for reading material from the royal archives and include with the request a personal message of her own.

The new lifestyle became a routine for Esther. The midmorning meals, the walks in the gardens, the daily dip in the swimming pool, and the beauty treatments. For six months, she lived this life, writing messages to Mordecai when she could and reading history and literature from the royal archives when her cousin sent scrolls, parchments, and clay tablets her way. By the time the first phase of the beauty treatments drew to a close, it seemed to Esther that an eternity had passed.

Then began the six months of perfumes and other cosmetics that were designed to make Esther more beautiful. Imports of aromatic cedar and pungent cypress made the treatments feel exotic, and the results were absolutely astonishing. Esther's attendants were generous with the frankincense and spikenard, but the process seemed so pointless to Hegai. Even the attending maidens had to admit that Esther looked as good without the eye shadows, rouges, and lip balms as she did with them.

Hegai was deeply impressed with Esther's natural beauty and reminded her of how fortunate she was. Her maidens knew that even in the morning, just out of bed, she looked radiant. By the time a year had passed, Esther was truly the most exquisite woman in all of Persia. Rumors about Esther came down from the harem to Mordecai.

And although he was not allowed to visit her in person, from time to time he did catch a glimpse of her when he came to the outer gate of the harem palace.

"God is watching over me," she tried to assure Mordecai and Bithiah when she wrote them letters, but she still worried about what it would be like to be married to the king. She did not want to be selected. The status and power of such a position was completely beyond her ambitions and capabilities. But what did the Lord God of her fathers want for her? Was it possible that she could be the wife or queen of a pagan king and still serve her God? It didn't seem likely.

CHAPTER 19

Esther sat at the large vanity table in her bedchamber, staring at her reflection in the large brass mirror on the wall. The late afternoon sun streamed through the open window, catching the sheen of her hair in its warm rays. As Parvona brushed Esther's long black locks, hints of iridescent blue rippled and danced across its shimmering surface. The big day Esther had been preparing for so long had finally come. Today she would finally meet the king.

She was wearing a rose-colored silk gown, with a white orchid fastened in her hair. That was it. To anyone looking on, the mirror was proof enough that Esther was indeed a wonderfully gorgeous woman! At Hegai's instruction, she was to wear no necklace or bracelets. No tiara. Nothing to distract the attention of the king. Just Esther in the simplicity of her own beauty.

"Are you ready for the big night, Esther?" A smile played across Hegai's usually serious face.

"No," she replied nervously. "If I had a hundred years to prepare, I don't really think I'd ever be ready!"

But during the weeks and months of waiting, Esther had grown more confident and more poised—and even more beautiful, if that were possible. Nervous as she was, Esther no longer thought of herself as Hadassah. The name was Esther now, and she was comfortable with it.

"Well now," Hegai raised his eyebrows. "I can see why you might be nervous, going to appear before the king, but we don't want to keep the king waiting, do we?"

She smiled at Hegai from her reflection in the mirror, "No, of course not." She turned to Hegai, and Parvona stopped brushing her hair. "You've been so kind, Hegai. Almost like a father to me." Hegai's hair had become streaked with gray, and she knew he was feeling his age.

"A father?" Hegai bowed his head humbly. "I'm honored. You've been like a daughter to me, too, Esther. It's been wonderful working with you, and I've spared no means to help get you where you are now." He lifted his head again and smiled matter-of-factly at her beautiful face. "Not that you needed any help."

Esther blushed and waved him off. She took one last look in the mirror and then stood to her feet. "Well, we might as well get the interview over with!" she announced dramatically. "Either he likes me, or he doesn't!"

"Here we go again," Hegai said in mock aggravation. "Honestly, Esther, what am I going to do with you? You've got every advantage I can think of, and a few more besides. He'll like you, Esther! Believe me, the king will like you! In fact, I'll wager that he'll be crazy about you! What other choice does he have?" He rolled his eyes. "You're the best and brightest this contest has turned up!"

Esther squirmed as she thought of the forty-six other young girls who had qualified as finalists and gone through the year-long preparation. Every one of them was stunning! It was the truth! When they were all in one room, anyone looking on might think them the most attractive group of beauty contestants ever assembled.

Now in its final stages, Hegai reminded Esther that the contest was to move through just a few more steps. First of all, the maidens were to be presented to the king as a group for his review. Then they would all eat the evening meal with him in the garden court of his royal palace. And then one-on-one visits with the king would begin so he could get to know the girls personally.

As the sun settled lower in the west, the palace guards from the royal citadel arrived to escort the girls to the evening event. Hegai and his crew of chamberlains went with them through the garden pathways and lamp-lit porticos, making sure they didn't snag their gowns on bushes or thorns along the way. What a sight the group of maidens made, walking along in their finery, stepping gingerly over the brick-paved pathways of the gardens, clicking along on the marble floors of the outer porticos. When they finally reached the massive bronze gate of the outer palace, Hegai lined them up so they could walk in single file.

"Are you scared?" the girl standing ahead of Esther asked. "I'm so nervous I could faint!" Her hands were shaking uncontrollably. Esther knew the girl had been having trouble biting her fingernails, and Hegai had scolded her countless times about it. At the moment, though, her nails looked immaculate.

Esther didn't know very many of the maidens. She had begun her preparations separate from them, and many she didn't remember having seen at all. But here they all were, standing at the gate to the citadel, ready to meet the most powerful man in the world. All of them were beautiful, and Esther couldn't imagine how the king was going to make a choice about which one to choose as his queen. She had no idea what kind of look or personality the king preferred. Did he like tall girls? Did he want a girl who had a lively, winsome personality, or did he prefer shy? Did he like dark-haired girls or fair-skinned maidens or girls with big eyes and long eyelashes?

The big meeting with the king was scary, exhilarating, and nerve-racking all at the same time. Esther had imagined that the king's palace could be imposing, but she had never seen it, so her first visit to the royal citadel was intimidating, to say the least.

Everywhere in the palace portico were curtain hangings of white and blue linen, fastened with cords of purple to silver rings on marble pillars. Couches of gold and silver sat here and there on a mosaic pavement set with jade, amethyst, and mother-of-pearl. And the center of attraction was the king's throne. Esther had heard that the throne was made of alabaster and trimmed with pure gold, and now she saw that it was true.

Not surprisingly, the king himself was imposing! Esther couldn't remember ever having seen a more handsome man. His hair was tied back in elaborate braids. His dark eyes were as black as obsidian, and a golden ring hung from one ear. He didn't smile, and he didn't say anything as the girls were being introduced. He just sat on his throne with his elbows on the armrests, watching the girls as they passed before him. Esther was twenty-ninth in line.

As she paraded past his throne, she snuck a sideways glance at the magnificent man, and noticed him sit up straighter on his throne. *What have I done wrong?* she wondered. She tried to remember everything Hegai had told her. *Never turn your back to the king, never look the king in the eye, and never, ever speak unless you have been asked to speak.*

She had done none of the above, so what had happened? She wished Hegai were here so she could ask him what to do, but of course, he wasn't, so she just kept right on walking.

CHAPTER 20

After the girls had all been introduced to the king, they were led to the banquet hall. Oil lamps of a unique design allowed light to reflect off a sheet of silver placed behind each flame. There must have been a hundred of the lamps, and they lit the palace as if it were day.

The girls were all seated on a long raised dais to one side of the banquet room. Their couches were made of fine woods such as algum, sandalwood, and ebony and then inlaid with intricate gold or silver trimming. Others were inlaid with ivory, and some were made almost entirely of silver, but each was unique.

Esther didn't know why she and the other beauty contestants were given seats of such importance. After all, they were only young girls. Persian custom did not usually provide for seats of such status for women of any age. Usually women were given floor cushions to sit on, or else they simply knelt on the floor.

And then the entertainment began. Esther sat wide-eyed with the other girls as two lines of dancers streamed through parted curtains to the right and left of the banquet hall. Their dark skin and colorful costumes of red, blue, and yellow told Esther they were probably from some country to the south of the Great Sea. Bright plumes of decorative feathers seemed to sprout from their heads and backs, and strange drums and whistles accompanied their gyrations.

Next, acrobats arrived, jumping and flipping in time with the music. A parade of exotic animals and birds were led in right behind them, adding flare and excitement to the show. Apes and peacocks and bright-feathered talking birds came next, giving everyone the picture of what it was like to live in the distant lands from where they came.

When the show had ended, Esther suddenly realized that she was hungry. Actually, ravenous was more like it. She had been nervous all day about this evening event, and now she felt she could finally begin to relax. There was no doubt that the entertainers had had something to do with that.

Again Esther grew wide-eyed at the banquet of unusual appetizers that were now brought out on silver and golden platters. Most of the banquet items were nothing more than sweet pastries and vintage wines, neither of which Esther cared for. She kept waiting for the real food to arrive, but it never did. Pastries were the enemy of a young woman's waistline, and wine made people say stupid things. And this evening of all evenings, Esther wanted to avoid acting silly. Besides, everything her cousin Mordecai had taught her about drinking wine came to mind now. "Wine is a mocker," he always said, "and wine is the friend of every fool."

Esther almost laughed when she thought of her cousin Mordecai and his antics. When she was just a little girl, Mordecai would sometimes stagger around the house, acting like a drunken man, just to show her how foolish it looked. She tried to keep a straight face now, knowing that she was in the banquet hall of the royal palace. Everything was on the line. She was sure it would be no small thing to see people getting drunk in the royal palace, and yet it would be kind of funny.

Fortunately, the king and his few advisors and honored guests didn't drink much, and before the hour was late, he dismissed the young maidens. Tomorrow was a big day, and they all needed to get their beauty rest, as Hegai put it so well.

Esther returned to her suite in the harem complex and slept late the next morning. When she finally did awaken, Parvona was pulling the filmy curtains aside from her windows.

"Well, well, sleepyhead," she giggled. "There's no rush for you to meet the day. They've listed you as twenty-fourth in line to see the king personally. That should give you plenty of time to get ready to meet the most important man in the world."

For more than two weeks, there was no word from the royal palace. Esther waited nervously, and then a message finally came that the king wished to see her. She was to prepare herself and show up at the king's inner palace that very evening.

When the announcement came, Esther's worries began all over again. Would the king like her? Would she be beautiful enough for him to choose as his queen? Would she be able to be herself and remain true to the standards of her God, the ones her cousin Mordecai had raised her with?

One thing she did know. She had been preparing for this day all her life, and now it had arrived. The months since she had first entered the harem had come and gone, and now it appeared that everything would change again. It was clear to Esther that she was going to become a wife of the king. There was no denying it any longer, but strangely enough, she had peace in her heart about the whole thing.

After the noonday rest period, Hegai came to Esther's suite to help her prepare. Under Hegai's supervision, her maidens gave her all the usual treatments with lotions and oils. They combed her hair, applied all the right mixtures of perfumes, and chose a blue silk gown with a wide sash for her to wear. In Hegai's opinion, Esther was the most beautiful of all the contestants, and he told her so. She did look stunning indeed—and all this at just seventeen years of age!

When the hour arrived, the guards came to escort her to the royal palace. Hegai went along for moral support, but the two said little on the way there. He had been very kind to her, but she probably would see him very seldom in the future—or perhaps not at all.

When they came to the giant bronze gates of the royal citadel, she turned to Hegai and said Goodbye. Tears came to her eyes, but she blinked them back and waved to him as the gate opened and then shut behind her.

CHAPTER 21

With great fanfare, Esther was ushered into the king's private living quarters. The place was lavish beyond description. She had heard amazing tales of the king's private chambers, but what she saw now left her speechless. The place was huge! As she entered the receiving room, the first things she saw were two sets of staircases that led to an upper level. The stairs were overlaid in ivory, and beside each step were golden bulls with human heads.

Between the two staircases was a full-sized tree made of solid gold. Across the expansive ceiling stretched an elaborate vine of gold, complete with leaves and bunches of grapes. Esther had to stop herself from gaping openmouthed at all the wonders.

She was escorted past the staircases and into the dining area, which was dimly lit with golden lamps. A fountain splashed from a floor-level pool, and songbirds warbled from golden cages.

A large round table, surrounded by deep plush cushions, sat low to the floor in the very center of the room. A palace attendant settled Esther on the cushions, where she waited. She glanced around her in awe. Everything was just right—the lighting, the perfumed air, and the furniture.

And then the king came in.

Esther had never been this close to royalty, let alone the most powerful ruler in the world. She had seen him more than two weeks before at his first meeting with all the beauty contestants, but now it made her head swim just to be near him. Tall and handsome with finely braided hair and beard, the king wore a smile that made her blush. She had worried about this meeting alone with him and could not keep from trembling. She had heard stories about his temper, that he could be a hard man when it came to punishing courtiers who failed to please him, but right now he was being a gentleman. Whatever the truth about such matters, this evening he was a master at helping her be herself. In seemingly no time at all, her fear had vanished.

The food this evening was a complete meal, more like a banquet than the refreshments the young women had been served during their previous visit to the king. All the food looked wonderful and smelled delicious.

Before they began eating, Dariush, the king's taster, came in to sample everything the king would be served. It was one of the many ways to make sure the king wouldn't be poisoned. If an assassination were to be attempted during a meal, it would most likely be done using poison made from an herb such as hemlock or from mushrooms. Several kings in the history of Persia had died this way, and Dariush's job was to make sure that Xerxes wasn't added to their ranks.

After Dariush left, King Xerxes began eating the delicacies served up on the golden platters. There were little cuts of meat and cheese on bite-sized bits of bread, fruit custards garnished with berries, and barbequed saltwater fish on skewers.

Esther smelled everything before she tasted it, and like Dariush, sampled the delicacy with minced bites before swallowing it. That was the only safe way to be sure she wasn't eating nonkosher food. Jews were limited in what they could eat according to the laws of Moses, which had been given to God's people clear back at Sinai. Esther realized that if ever there was a time for someone to eat whatever was placed before them, the time would be now.

But she also knew her ties to Jehovah were stronger than anything else in the world. Her loyalties and allegiance to the God of her fathers was more important than all the evenings in the world with all the kings of all the earth. That kind of talk sounded brave, and on the outside Esther looked the part, but inside she was quaking.

The king's wine was served in golden goblets, but Esther had previously decided that she wouldn't drink any of it. It had no doubt been dedicated to the gods of Persia, and that alone made it off-limits to her as a Jewess. She wasn't sure how she could avoid offending the king if she explained it that way, especially since he didn't know her people were from Judah. But there were other reasons for not drinking the wine too. She was young and a bit worried about what might happen if she drank too much of the ruby-red liquid.

This was a very special evening. Here she was eating dinner with the mighty King Xerxes. The last thing she wanted to do was become dizzy or black out, and she worried that this was exactly what would happen. She wasn't used to drinking wine, so she didn't know how much she could drink and still stay sober. And, of course, her cousin Mordecai's words came to mind, "Wine is a mocker." Right now, she knew she looked beautiful and flowerlike, and she wanted to stay that way. She hoped the king wouldn't mind, and as she smiled sweetly at him, she could tell by the look on his face that he didn't object to her decision.

Siavash, the king's personal priest, came by to give the couple his blessing. He didn't stay long. Just long enough to officially pronounce Esther as the new bride of King Xerxes. It was all very lovely and very solemn in the way it was done. Esther wished one of the Jewish elders could have been there to give them Jehovah's blessing, but of course, that was not possible.

The rest of the evening flew by. She was nervous, but as long as she lived, she would never forget this first night as a royal wife in the palace of the king. It was perfect! The king listened to her and laughed with her and made her feel important. And he adored her. It was obvious the way he kept looking at her. There was no other way to put it. She didn't think he could love her yet. He didn't even know her personally, but he liked her, and that was enough for now. Love could grow from that wonderful start.

And she knew she would learn to love him too. Women didn't usually marry for love in Persia. As was the custom of the day, they were bartered for cattle, land, and booty seized in battle. Xerxes was a pagan king, and she couldn't change that, but she prayed, asking that the God of heaven would help the king learn to love her.

The thought that King Xerxes must still choose a queen from among the many finalists in the competition hardly entered Esther's mind on this splendid evening. Even if he didn't choose her to become his queen, it didn't matter. At seventeen years of age, she was now the wife of the most powerful man in the world, and that was overwhelming enough.

CHAPTER 22

Two weeks passed, and Esther tried to keep herself busy. She would continue to live in separate quarters from the king, as all the wives did. She had no illusions about what it would be like to be married to a king—at least she hoped she didn't. She wouldn't be able to see the king whenever she wanted—only when he asked specifically to see her. That could be often—or hardly ever.

This is the way it was in the Persian court. She didn't like it, and it wasn't the way family life was taught in the books of Moses—but there was nothing she could do about it. She would never have said such things out loud, but she could think them. It was one thing Aunt Bithiah had taught her well.

Then, of course, Xerxes was the most powerful ruler in the world. Everyone in the Persian court treated Xerxes as if he were a god, as if he had fallen out of the sky one day. She knew he wasn't a god, but he did have the power to do whatever he wanted, and that in itself was a solemn thought. Esther knew her loyalties lay in being the wife of the king, but she would never worship him. He was her king and her husband, but not her god. Jehovah was the only real God for her.

The next day Hegai stopped by for a visit. "Is there anything I can get you?" he asked. "Now that you are officially the king's wife, I won't be responsible for you anymore, but I'd still like to come by now and then, if you don't mind."

"Yes, of course, please do. You know I don't mind." Esther smiled fondly at this man who had been such a help in getting her through the past year. And he had been a good friend too.

"You know, you always were my favorite of all the maidens in the group." He smiled almost shyly. "It was your gentle ways and sweet smile, I think. At first I thought it was your beauty, but as I got to know you, I knew it was much more than that." He bowed his head in respect. "You'll not forget me, will you?"

"Forget you? Of course not, Hegai! How could I forget you?" Esther stated in amazement. "You showed me kindness when I hadn't a friend in the palace but Droxshana. You can come by to check on me anytime." Her words seemed to be enough assurance for him.

"So how is the king coming along in his search for a queen?" she changed the subject.

Hegai smiled at Esther's polite conversation. "I haven't heard much, except that he has stopped asking for any other young maidens to come dine with him." He could tell she was more than just a little bit interested in the answer he might give.

Esther looked worried. "What's the matter? Is he sick?"

"I don't know. I'm not his personal physician." Hegai grinned boyishly.

"Oh, you know what I mean!" Esther shook a finger at him. "Is everything all right? Has he received word from the army to the west? I've heard he'll soon begin another war with the Greeks."

"Can't say. I don't know, but if I did, and when I do, you'll be the first to know. I'm not that important around here, you know. I don't hear everything that goes on."

"You hear a lot more than most, Hegai."

"I can't deny that," he added with a smile of confidence.

But that afternoon, Esther got a lovely shock. The quiet serenity of the harem palace was suddenly interrupted by a buzz of excitement as Shaashgaz appeared, knocking excitedly at the door of her suite. "Esther! Esther! I have the most wonderful news for you! The king wants to see you again. He's asking that you come for a banquet this evening. Scores of important officials will be there, and you, Esther, are to be the guest of honor!" Shaashgaz bowed politely, as he tried to catch his breath.

"The guest of honor? Me?" Esther turned to greet Shaashgaz, her face flushed with excitement, and then she remembered that she didn't need to blush anymore. She was the wife of the king. Of course, some things would never change for her. Even though she was the wife of the most powerful man in the world, there was a small part of her that was still a little girl inside.

That she was to be the guest of honor at an evening banquet meant something, but what exactly, she hadn't a clue. The king didn't probably need a particular reason for inviting her to dine with him at his evening banquets. After all, he was the king.

But she still wondered. She reminded herself that she didn't need to worry. Whatever it was, she was sure it would be good. She was the king's wife, and it felt good knowing that. Maybe she would even tell him someday about her family background, that she was a Jewess, and that she loved and worshiped Jehovah, the One True God of heaven and earth. Maybe—but not now. God would let her know when the time was right, but until then, it would be her secret.

Shaashgaz helped Esther prepare for the evening. All Esther's maidens were called in to help prepare her bath and get her blue silk gown ready. They added rose petals and perfume of spikenard to her bathwater. And when they had finished her grooming, there wasn't a more beautiful woman in all of God's creation.

CHAPTER 23

And then to everyone's surprise, Mehuman, the king's chief chamberlain, came to the harem to deliver a diamond necklace. Everyone stopped to stare in awe at the dozens of special cut diamonds. "Now that is a fine piece of royal jewelry!" Shaashgaz gasped. "It's even finer than anything Queen Vashti ever wore!"

Esther caught her breath as she saw the diamonds catch the late afternoon sunlight. A thousand, thousand little lights refracted from the little prisms. Never had she imagined that she would wear something like this. It all seemed so wrong and impossibly vain to have such jewelry in her wardrobe.

Even so, she smiled at the reflection of herself in the polished bronze mirror of her vanity table. She didn't think she really needed the necklace for beauty's sake. As Cousin Mordecai had told her a hundred times before, her real beauty was in her eyes and skin. These were the features that gave her appeal as a young maiden.

But what could she do? The king had sent her the necklace to wear, and one did not argue about such things with the most powerful king in the world. "It's beautiful!" Esther *oohed* and *aahed* with the others as she took one last look at herself in the mirror. Then she stood to her feet and glided across the dressing room floor, her attendants following close behind.

The evening had a chilly nip to it, but Shaashgaz had thought of everything. As they left the harem complex, he placed a deep-blue shawl of fine mohair around Esther's shoulders and let her adjust it to her liking. Then he clapped his hands, and a parade of guards fell in beside them to escort the party to the royal palace banquet hall.

It didn't take long to reach the east wing of the citadel, and when they arrived at the tall bronze gates, the feast was already in full swing. Everyone who was anyone was there—nobles and officials from every local government, army generals, satraps, provincial magistrates, soothsayers, magicians, astrologers, and advisors. Even a few prestigious guests from foreign lands were present. King Xerxes' brother Achaemenes was among the guests, as was an ambassador from Greece, and five or six royal officials from Ethiopia.

But when Esther's retinue of attendants entered the banquet hall, a hush slowly settled on the waiting crowd. The king turned on his golden couch covered with red and blue cushions to see Esther. And when he caught sight of her, he did the most remarkable thing! So enchanted was he with this lovely young woman, now his bride of only a few days, that he stood and bowed in her direction. Esther would later learn that King Xerxes had never before bowed to anyone except his father, the former king of Persia.

The king remained on his feet, which was out of character for him too. Persian kings prided themselves on the formality of court life. They never stood to honor anyone's presence but their own, and yet here he was, obviously forgetting himself in the excitement of the moment as he gazed on Esther's face.

Court musicians began playing soft music as the king lifted his hand and gestured toward the beautiful Esther. She was alone now. Her attendants had backed away, leaving her standing in the middle of the royal great hall.

"I wish to welcome everyone here tonight for this very special occasion!" the king called in trumpetlike tones, not taking his eyes off Esther. "On this night, the royal court has some very important news to announce!"

Esther smiled. It was obvious the king was trying to be formal, but it seemed she could tell he was not his usual self. In fact, it surprised her that he should be making the announcement himself at all. She was sure that such things were usually handled by court officials. She didn't know the king that well, but she thought his eyes had an unusual light in them as they had on their first evening together.

"I have come to the end of my search for a new queen!" the king continued. "As you know, we've been planning and working toward this for well over a year now. Beautiful maidens from the farthest corners of my kingdom have been brought to the court to be considered for the honor, and, just this morning, I finally made my choice!"

Esther's heart fell a little. She had hoped that her marriage to the king had been enough to win his favor, but now it appeared that someone else would have first place in his heart and in the hearts of the court officials. *Why did I allow myself to get my hopes up in the first place?* Esther asked herself. *I should have known better! Cousin Mordecai tried to warn me that the chances of being chosen as queen were very slim indeed.*

CHAPTER 24

The king paused and glanced at Esther. It was almost as if he had heard her thoughts, and the impression frightened her. She had let her mind drift, and now she suddenly snapped back to the reality of the ceremony at hand. How dare she allow herself to lose focus on the king! Had he asked her a question? If he had, she wouldn't know how to answer it because she hadn't been listening! Would he be angry? Would he have one of his temper tantrums? Might he banish her as he had Queen Vashti? What would happen next?

But wait! The king was smiling and speaking again, and he was looking directly at her! "The search is over!" the king continued. "To my great surprise, we found exactly what I had been looking for in a queen right here at home in the royal city of Susa!" He lifted his right hand. "I want to praise all the gods of Persia for this magnificent answer to my prayers." He paused. "And if there be any unknown God out there, let Him be praised also, because He has done a marvelous thing for me this day. This God has answered my heart's every desire and given me a woman I can truly love."

It was a very moving speech, and the audience was hushed now as the king's emotions seemed to take over, capturing every heart. The king continued staring at Esther, and it began to make her feel uncomfortable. From the corners of her eyes, she could see that everyone in the banquet hall was looking at her too. *Why are they staring at me?* she wondered. *Is there something wrong with my gown or my hair or the necklace the king asked me to wear?*

"Loyal subjects and honored quests!" the king was still speaking, jarring Esther once again from a trance. "I'm pleased to announce that I've selected Esther to be my new queen!"

Esther glanced around her uncomprehending. *What did the king say? Who has he selected to be his next queen?* The crowd was smiling at her now, but it didn't make sense. And then it hit her— he had said she was the new queen! Surely she hadn't heard right! Was she dreaming? Was she really to be the new queen of the Persian Empire! She was already the king's new bride, but was she now to be the new queen, as well?

Esther could faintly hear the crowd's applause. Everything was in a blur as a court attendant came forward holding a silk pillow. On it was a most exquisite tiara, delicately crafted with a bridge of diamonds arching up to a pointed crest. The band around the bottom of the tiara was set with scores of small emeralds to match the very color of her eyes. She couldn't comprehend it all at the time, but later she would look back in awe at how wonderful the whole ceremony must have appeared.

The king himself, with his own hands, placed the crown on her head. He did it with pride and adoration, and though Esther didn't know him well, she thought she would probably never see him this flushed again. According to everything she had heard about Persian kings, they just didn't get this informal!

A place of honor had been prepared for Esther beside the king's couch. The new bride was now his new queen. Her couch was a bit smaller than his, but just as exquisite, made from solid gold, with pomegranates and fig leaves sculpted into the legs and backrest. Large lavender cushions with roses stitched in gold thread gave the reclining couch a soft, truly inviting appearance.

No talk of future battles or conquest in foreign lands was made on this evening. No talk of alliances with kings abroad. The time seemed to be all hers. The banquet truly was being held in her honor.

King Xerxes looked so pleased to have her there. It was as if she were the only person in the whole wide world. He took her hand in his and led her to the golden couch with lavender cushions. Her maiden attendants then stepped forward to help arrange the flowing folds of her gown on the couch. And with that musicians struck a new chord as the party sailed on into the night.

It was a glorious feast. The king enjoyed himself so much that before the evening was through, he declared the next three days a national holiday. All businesses in Susa were to be closed, and each loyal subject was commanded to sacrifice a goat to his god, with the chief honors being given to King Xerxes himself, of course. In celebration, the people were asked to burn a cone of incense in the worship of His Royal Highness and then drink to the king's health.

As the guests left the royal feast that night, all received generous gifts from the king. Gold medallions were handed out to everyone in honor of the new Queen Esther. The ambassador from Greece was given a shield of gold that Esther guessed must have weighed at least five thousand shekels. The Ethiopian officials were given one of Xerxes' royal ships on which they could sail home to the land of Cush. Prince Achaemenes, the most honored and prestigious guest, was given a beautiful princess to be his wife.

CHAPTER 25

The next morning Esther awoke to the sound of birds. She could hear the little sparrows in the vines that crawled up the latticework of the trellis just outside her window. Now and then, she caught the faint chirping of indigo swallows as they swooped back and forth in their search for flying insects. But most obvious of all were the noisy red-and-blue parrots squawking among the exotic plants of the garden walkways outside her window.

As Esther lay in her bed, she watched the sunbeams dancing playfully on the ceiling, reflections from the lotus pool at the center of her palace garden. She loved the way the little circles of light skipped and jumped on the ivory mosaics of the ceiling above her bed. It gave her a feeling of peace and tranquility and took her back to the simpler days of childhood.

About midmorning, after she had eaten a meal of yogurt with a piece of toasted wheat bread on the side, a courier arrived with a message from Cousin Mordecai. It was fastened with the usual wax seal. "My little star, congratulations on your new appointment!" she read from the tightly rolled parchment. "I'm overwhelmed that you have been chosen for such a position, but I'm not surprised. Not really. You, above all girls in Persia, deserve the honor."

Mordecai had not taken pains to be careful in his wording. Evidently, he was not concerned that the parchment could fall into the wrong hands.

"I've been given a promotion too," he continued. "I'm now going to be working as the scribe who records the guests that come and go at the main gate to the inner palace. I'm tempted to believe it has something to do with your new appointment. How else it could have happened, I can't imagine, but I know that's not possible. You've managed to keep your identity a secret, and you couldn't have done that if they had known I was your cousin. You've kept your promise, Hadassah, and I must commend you for it. It took courage for you to leave home and go live in a palace where Jehovah is not reverenced or worshiped. May the God of our fathers keep you safe as the new queen of the great and mighty Xerxes."

A new chamberlain came to work for Esther at this time. Hatach, personal attendant to King Xerxes, was now to be her assistant—a wedding present from the royal citadel. He was to be her own private courier to take messages wherever they needed to go on the palace grounds. He was also to screen all her visitors and make all the arrangements when she wanted to attend the various parties, banquets, and political events that were a part of royal life.

Even so, in the days that followed, Esther still called on Hegai from time to time. Sometimes, she would ask him how the other finalists from the beauty contest were doing. He told her that many had already qualified as wives for King Xerxes, but that some had not been chosen.

"How about Droxshana?" Esther dared to ask. "Is she to be in the harem now too?"

Knowing what friends the two girls had been, Hegai spoke reluctantly. "I'm sorry, Your Highness, but she wasn't chosen."

"That's too bad." Esther got a faraway look in her eye. "I would have thought for sure she would be one of the girls chosen. She has such a pleasant personality." Esther plotted her next move. "Hmm, I was wondering," she added, "do you think it would be

possible for Droxshana to come and work here as one of my attendants in the royal suite? She has always meant so much to me
as a friend, and this would be the least I could do for her. If you
think she would be willing?" Esther quickly added.

"She would be honored to serve you here," Hegai said respectfully. "I'll see that she receives the message, but I'll need to move
quickly on it. I believe she is scheduled to go home in a few
days."

Within a week, the chamberlains moved Esther again, this
time to the suite of rooms that had been Vashti's. It was only
right that she have the best, Shaashgaz told her. "After all, you
are the queen, Your Highness."

The number and size of the rooms in the suite were even more
sumptuous than the ones Esther had been given in the harem
when she first arrived. How this could be possible was a wonder
to Esther. She already had more space than she knew what to do
with, but then again, that was the way of royalty! That was how
things were supposed to be when you were the queen.

Months passed and Esther settled into a routine at the palace.
Surprisingly enough, being the new queen of Persia didn't require
much from Esther. Sometimes she was asked to entertain the
wives of government officials and foreign ambassadors who came
to the palace. Banquets and receptions in the royal gardens of
Susa were also regular events.

Shaashgaz, Hatach, and sometimes even Hegai, would help
her plan the events. These chamberlains made all the arrangements for the parties, but they never made her feel as if she were
a child. They realized that she was young and still learning the
rituals and ceremonies of the palace. Esther knew that soon she
was going to have to take more responsibility, but right now she
was content to let Shaashgaz tend to all the details.

CHAPTER 26

One evening, Hatach entered the royal harem and knocked on the doors of Esther's private suite. He found her curled up on a couch in her receiving room, reading from a scroll of Babylonian poetry.

"I've been asked to deliver this message from the palace." Hatach's expression was serious as he bowed. "It's from Mordecai, a scribe at the king's gate." Esther could see that the parchment had an official wax seal attached to ensure the security of its contents. "If it pleases the queen, Mordecai has asked that I stay by and wait for a return message."

Esther broke the seal, and as she read the message, her eyes widened. Jumping to her feet, she asked, "When did Mordecai give this to you?"

"Just now!" Hatach replied. "He asked that I come to you immediately, that it was a matter of palace security."

Esther drew a quick breath. "Well, it certainly is! Do you know what this message is about?"

Hatach raised both hands in protest. "Your Highness, how could I know what is in the message? I would have had to break the seal to find out."

"No—of course you wouldn't know what's in the scroll! I apologize." Esther assured him. "But according to this message from Mordecai, a plot is taking shape to assassinate the king, and

Mordecai has information that reveals who the instigators are."

Hatach's eyes were wide now too. "How did he find out such a thing?" he gasped.

Esther scanned the parchment again. "Evidently, a young slave boy overheard two chamberlains talking about the plot on the king. The slave boy is a waiter in the servants' dining quarters where the men were eating their noonday meal. He must have come to Mordecai because he knew Mordecai was a gatekeeper and security scribe in the palace."

"Does the message say when or where this is supposed to happen?"

"Mordecai doesn't say anything about the time or location." Esther's mind was whirling. "But we can probably guess where. If it's two chamberlains making the plans, it will probably happen in the king's bedchamber while he's sleeping!"

Hatach's expression changed to wonder and awe. "Well, I never would have guessed it, Your Highness! You are new to the palace, and already you've probably helped unravel some of the details of the plot!"

Esther immediately sat down to write a message to the king and another one to Mordecai. "Does anyone else know about this message from Mordecai?"

"Not that I know of."

"Good. Then take this message to the king and alert his personal bodyguard." Esther rolled up the fresh parchment. "Tell the king I sent it personally!" She pressed her official seal to the melted wax on the scroll and handed it to Hatach. "Don't let anyone else see this. Don't stop to talk to anyone on the way to the citadel. Don't entrust it to the keepers of the door to his private quarters—and especially not to his chamberlains. It appears that some of them may be in on the conspiracy, so ask to read the message personally when you arrive in the presence of the king! This is a matter of royal security!" Esther had begun pacing the floor. "And please, Hatach, bring me word as to what the king says!"

"Yes, Your Highness!"

"And be sure the king understands it was Mordecai who uncovered the plot!" Esther called after Hatach, as he hurried out the door.

Esther wished there was something more she could do, but she knew that was impossible. Wives of the king were not invited to go to the royal palace even in times of emergency. Without an invitation, that part of the palace complex was off-limits. Esther knew she had done as much as she could. Now she would simply have to wait to see what would happen next.

But even after Hatach had gone, Esther continued pacing. She kept looking out the window toward the west wing of the citadel, where she knew Hatach would be speaking to the king shortly. *What will the king do?* she worried. *Will he discover the guilty ones in time and have them punished?*

She tried to imagine the expression on the king's face when he read the message about the assassination plot. *Will he understand the part Mordecai has played in uncovering the scheme? Will he reward Mordecai and the slave boy in the kitchen who came forward with the critical information?* Esther hoped so. Though it must have been only a few hours, the waiting seemed like an eternity!

When one of Esther's royal chamberlains came in carrying some fresh towels, she asked him to deliver a message to her cousin. "Take this directly to Mordecai in the inner gate of the king's palace," she told the chamberlain, and then had a sudden thought that terrified her. *Will word somehow get back to the assassins that Mordecai had been the one to alert the king? Might they try to waylay him on his way home this evening?* "Also, tell Mordecai not to leave his post at the king's gate until he hears from me again," she added.

CHAPTER 27

The next morning, the royal harem was in an uproar. Everybody was talking about the assassination plot against the king. All day long servants came and went, bringing the latest news from the citadel. Before sunset, word came to Esther that the two guilty parties had been caught and sentenced to death for treason against the king.

"Their names are Bigthan and Teresh, two of the king's personal attendants," Shaashgaz said when he returned to the harem to see to the details of the evening meal. "Quite a pair they are! And to think that they were entrusted with the job of guarding the very doors to the king's sleeping chamber!"

Esther shuddered. "Is the king all right?" She began to relax a little, but she still felt uneasy. After all, it was her husband they were talking about.

"The king is fine, Your Highness." Shaashgaz assured her. "He's the king, and thanks to the message from Mordecai, he'll be the king for a very long time. Long live the king!" Shaashgaz gave Esther a polite bow, but then he frowned.

"Unfortunately, the crime is not completely solved. Bigthan and Teresh refused to confess who had hired them to assassinate the king. Whoever it was, he must have paid them handsomely." Shaashgaz gazed out the west window toward the citadel. "Bigthan and Teresh were ideal candidates for the job because they were guards at the door to the king's inner chambers. Let's just hope the king's bodyguard can get them to confess before they're executed."

Shaashgaz paused to give orders to the servants who were setting out the evening meal. "Spread a sky-blue cloth of silk on the queen's serving table, Sohrab, and while you're at it, why don't you move that silver urn of flowers nearer the window. And, Ashkan, remember to light the evening lamps."

The harem administrator turned to bow respectfully again at Esther. "And now I must be going. I need to tend to the evening meal, myself." He added one parting thought. "I will say one thing, Your Highness. I think the king is fortunate to have loyal subjects such as Mordecai in his palace. With men like Mordecai around, enemies will have a much more difficult time staging a rebellion and seizing the throne."

Esther thought about Bigthan and Teresh. She thought about their assassination plot gone wrong. How close had they come to actually pulling it off? Days? Hours? The money they had been paid to plan and carry out the deed wouldn't do them any good now because they were scheduled to be executed at high noon the next day.

* * * *

The next day dawned clear, and it promised to be hot in the courtyard where the executions were scheduled to take place. The king was there, dressed in his finest royal robes. He even wore a two-tiered crown on his head. Satraps and governors, magistrates, counselors, and wise men were all invited to witness the executions of the decade. Everyone who was anyone came, including Esther, who had been the one to pass the warning on to the king. Strangely enough, Mordecai wasn't there. In fact, he

hadn't even been invited as Esther later found out, and that baf-
fled her. *Was it a mistake? Had a courier forgotten to deliver the
invitation?* When Esther really thought about it, she realized that
she should not have been surprised. After all, Mordecai was only
a scribe, someone who recorded the comings and goings of visitors to the palace.

But still, it didn't seem right. The fact that there would have
been no executions at all without Mordecai's quick message of
warning to the king was somehow lost in the whirlwind of excitement. It seemed obvious to Esther that Mordecai should have
been the honored guest, but, of course, her opinion didn't count
in the politics of the citadel. She was living in a man's world, even
if she was the queen.

Not surprisingly, a canopy had to be erected to shelter the
overflow of guests. The palace overseer had planned for over three
hundred guests, but there ended up being almost five hundred,
and they came dressed in their royal robes of scarlet, blue, or deep
purple.

Adding to the festive atmosphere, the palace administrator
made sure the guests were provided refreshments. Wine from
the king's own stock was brought out, and barbequed meats were
abundant. The food smelled good, but even in the sumptuous
surroundings of the palace, it was impossible to keep the bugs
away. Bees came to sample the sweet wine, and flies showed up,
attempting to get a share of the roasted pork. But it didn't seem
to bother the guests much. Everyone was too focused on the approaching moment of the executions to pay much attention to
insects or the heat.

When the royal trumpets began sounding, Esther knew the
awful moment had come. She watched in silence as Bigthan and
Teresh were dragged from a prison door in the courtyard wall.
They had come to their last day of life, and she trembled for their

souls! They did not know the God of Abraham, Isaac, and Jacob. They did not serve the Living God, who could save them from their pagan lives steeped in anger, hate, and vengeance.

But the crowd of imperial visitors had other plans for the would-be assassins. As the royal executioners impaled Bigthan and Teresh on wooden stakes, the crowd went wild. They cheered and jeered, calling the two men all kinds of hateful things.

It was an awful sight, and Esther cringed as she listened to the two men curse at their executioners and scream in pain. Fortunately, they soon died from loss of blood, ending their misery. Esther breathed a sigh of relief when it was all over. The men had been executed justly, but watching them die was horrifying.

CHAPTER 28

In the month of Iyyar, Esther received another invitation to come to a banquet provided by the royal palace. As usual, she dressed in her best finery, and Droxshana was there to help. True to his word, Hegai had arranged for Droxshana to be one of Esther's personal attendants. That made eight maidens-in-waiting now.

It was wonderful having Droxshana around to help all the time. Esther always felt so relaxed when the two of them were together. Droxshana was cheerful, positive, and gentle. With her smile, she had a way of making every problem seem simple, every day seem glorious. And now when Esther needed advice about what to wear for occasions such as this banquet, Droxshana was there to offer suggestions.

The sun was beginning to set when Esther arrived at the royal banquet hall, and, as usual, she caused quite a stir. The saffron-colored gown she wore with a silk sash over her shoulder made her the picture of perfection.

But the banquet wasn't being held in Esther's honor, so she remained in the background in an alcove to one side of the raised dais where the king sat on his throne. From all the fanfare, it soon became evident the king wished to honor Haman, one of the advisors of the court and a longtime friend of King Xerxes with the promotion to a new position in the empire—prime minister over all of Persia.

Esther didn't know Haman well, but from what she had heard from Mordecai and read in the royal archives, he was a descendant of King Agag, an enemy of the Israelites some sixteen generations back. That had been in the days of the great prophet Samuel, nearly six hundred years before.

Haman looked to be such an arrogant man. Esther knew in her heart that although she was an important woman in the palace of the king now, Haman was much more important. Haman had known the king for longer than she had—they were such good friends, it seemed. She could not afford to get on the wrong side of this man. His eyes were too cold and calculating. She could imagine that if his anger were ever aroused, he would probably be cruel as well, an enemy she could not afford to have.

And she was right. A week later, her suspicions were aroused when Hegai came by for a visit. "What's troubling you, Hegai?" Esther asked. She knew Hegai hadn't come by her suite by accident. He looked upset, and she was sure he felt she would listen.

"I'm worried, Your Highness," he confessed quietly. He glanced around the receiving room to check for eavesdroppers and then lowered his voice even more. "The new prime minister is getting power hungry, and those of us in the palace are beginning to feel the sting of it. It's already getting out of hand."

"Getting out of hand?"

Hegai's eyes narrowed. "It's like this. When Haman walks through the palace grounds, he expects everyone to bow as he passes."

"That's getting out of hand?" Esther asked in surprise. "Lots of the king's officials do that."

"Not like Haman, they don't. Take me, for example. As director of the beauty pageant and manager of the king's personal business, when I pass in the corridors or streets, I get respect enough from the palace servants and guards. They bow their heads and even sometimes bow from the waist. And that's enough for me. It's fine. A royal official deserves respect. But this Haman? He treats everyone as if they are slaves—or even worse, lepers. I've watched him many times in action! Sometimes he makes people get down and kiss his feet as he passes. One time I even saw him force a palace servant's face to the ground and then put his foot on the man's neck and held him there for a while."

Hegai shook his head again. "I have a very bad feeling about Haman. When he gets it in his head that he doesn't like someone, he'll stop at nothing to humiliate him!" Hegai glanced around before adding, "Let me give you an idea of what I'm talking about. There's a scribe at the main gate to the king's inner palace. His name is Mordecai. You remember him. He's a good man. He's the one who helped uncover the plot to assassinate the king. Anyway, there isn't a day that passes that he doesn't say something kind to me when we meet, and he's always helping sort out problems among the servants in the palace.

"But Haman doesn't like Mordecai, and everybody knows it. All the other servants in the palace, and even the officers, bow to Haman when he passes, but not Mordecai. He says he can't because his religion won't allow it." Hegai was frowning now. "I'm concerned for men like Mordecai, Your Highness. I'm concerned for all of us. One doesn't always receive justice in Susa, and with Haman in charge, things can only get worse."

Esther listened quietly to Hegai's mention of Mordecai. Obviously, Hegai had no idea of her relationship to Mordecai. She thought about Hegai's words, and she thought about Mordecai's advice that she not reveal her true identity. She was glad now that she had obeyed him and kept her secret about being Jewish. And she knew it must stay that way. But she would have to be doubly careful now. It was the only way to be safe.

But she was also worried about Mordecai. What was he thinking when he refused to bow down to the powerful new prime minister? Jews were in the habit of giving respect to government officials of all kinds, especially when the official held the higher position. *But this must be different,* Esther reasoned. *Otherwise, Cousin Mordecai wouldn't be drawing attention to himself like this.* He had to have a good reason. He was smart, and he was a worshiper of Jehovah. She trusted him.

Hegai was bowing to Esther now. "If it pleases the queen, I'll be going. I just stopped briefly while on an errand."

"Thank you, Hegai. Keep me posted." Esther watched him go, but was afraid to say much more. But she was glad to hear the news about her cousin anyway, especially if it meant he might be in some kind of trouble and needed help.

After Hegai had gone, Esther sat down and wrote Mordecai a message, asking for more information. What were his intentions in refusing to bow to Haman? What could happen if he didn't? Should he be more worried for his safety?

Later that afternoon, she asked one of the chamberlains to deliver the parchment to Mordecai with some other messages being sent to the gate of the king. The next morning, a message came back, and what Mordecai told her made sense. Haman was not only asking everyone to bow to him, he was demanding that they lay down their coats for him to walk on as he passed by in the corridors and walkways of the palace gardens. He was also commanding them to offer up prayers to him as he rode by on his chariot in the streets of Susa.

"I see trouble coming," Mordecai warned Esther, "but I don't think there's a lot we can do about it. We must pray that God will protect us from this evil man."

Esther thought some more about what Hegai had said. He was right. In a Persian city like Susa, there was little justice! Life was not fair. If you weren't born into a wealthy family or didn't know someone important, there was little chance you would ever get ahead. And if someone in a position of power such as Haman didn't like you, things could get even worse. He could charge you with some horrible crime and then put you in prison—or even have you executed.

She knew that in Judah, the Torah had provided a system of justice for her people. Not that justice was always carried out, but at least people knew what was right, and there were courts to which one could appeal. The Law of Moses made it all very clear.

But Esther was not in Judah. She was in Persia, and she must live under the laws of this pagan land. "Please, Lord," she prayed. "Cousin Mordecai is in trouble, and I don't know what to do for him. He is very brave. Honor him for being true to You, Lord. He has been a faithful servant of the Most High. May he live long and prosper."

CHAPTER 29

As the days went by, things got worse. Now that Haman was prime minister in the court, a new tale of bad news circulated every day.

One afternoon, Esther was sitting on her royal-blue reading couch with several of her maidens around her, tending her hair, skin, and nails. Parvona was brushing Esther's long dark curls, Kahin and Keshvar were giving her one of their famous skin treatments, and Morvari had just brought in a fresh batch of scented oils.

Out in the receiving room, she could hear two men speaking in hushed tones, and Mordecai's name kept coming up. Esther sat up a little straighter as she realized it was Hatach and Hegai.

From where she sat, Esther could see Hegai standing with his back to her. The two men's voices rose and fell on the warm afternoon air, but now and then, Esther caught snatches of what they were saying.

"Haman is up to no good, I tell you! He's a very powerful man! It's obvious he's out for blood, and Mordecai isn't helping much." That was Hegai's voice.

"In the name of the king, why doesn't he just bow the knee when Haman passes?" Hatach was shaking his head. "I know he has religious convictions to his God, but this is suicide! If he doesn't manage to appease Haman, I think his days are numbered!"

Esther's pulse quickened. She strained harder to catch every word they were saying. She wanted to ask the two men for all the details, but in some ways, it was better eavesdropping. This way the men would be more likely to say exactly what they were thinking.

"You're right about that, and it's a real shame too. Mordecai is respected by so many people, including the king!"

"How do you think Haman will get rid of him?" It was Hatach's voice again.

"Oh, one way or another, he'll manage. Have no doubt, if anyone in the royal court can find a way, Haman will!"

By the sound of things, Cousin Mordecai's predicament was getting worse, and Esther had to ask herself some very hard questions. *Was Mordecai being too stubborn for his own good? Was he being realistic when he refused to bow to Haman?*

She wanted to be part of the conversation so she could find out more about Mordecai, but she didn't want the two men to know Mordecai was her cousin. Then she came up with a plan.

"Gentlemen," she called, "am I to understand that this Mordecai you've been speaking of is in trouble with the prime minister? Is he the same scribe that uncovered the plot to assassinate the king?" She knew she needed to disguise her interest in the matter, or they might begin to put two and two together. *Will they hear the concern in my voice? Will they see the love in my eyes for this man who is like a father to me?*

The men hurried to where she sat with a parchment lying across her lap. "Yes, Your Highness," Hatach replied, bowing, "he's the one." He glanced at Hegai. "We're sorry to have disturbed you with such a matter. The day-to-day events of the palace should not concern you, Your Majesty."

"I'll decide what should and should not concern me, Hatach," came Esther's sharp reply. "In matters that involve the well-being of the king, I think I have a definite interest. Do I make myself clear?" Esther couldn't believe she had spoken to Hatach in such a manner. She couldn't remember when she had ever used that tone with him.

"Yes, Your Highness," he bowed again, his face turning red with embarrassment. "You are quite right, and it was foolish of me to think otherwise. I'll see that it doesn't happen again."

Her tone softened a bit, and a sparkling hint of a twinkle danced in her eye. "Your apology is accepted," she replied. "And now, about this Mordecai. Was anything ever done to reward him for his part in uncovering the plot to assassinate the king?"

Hatach looked at Hegai again, and then back to the queen. "I don't know, Your Highness, but I can find out."

"I'd like that. Please report back to me as soon as possible."

"Yes, Your Majesty!"

A few days later, Esther was invited to yet another banquet at which she met the prime minister again, this time at a much closer range. He bowed to her when she arrived, but his smile looked painted on, as though he were disguising the real feelings that hid beneath the surface.

Everything Esther had heard about this man could be seen in his face, and she knew that the trouble he could make for Cousin Mordecai was real indeed. *What plans does he have?* she wondered. When Haman took her hand to kiss it in respect, she wondered what he would say if he knew that Mordecai was her cousin. She studied his cold eyes and decided that he must be every bit as wicked as his reputation said he was.

* * * *

And then one morning, Hatach came in with more unsettling news from the palace. Haman was on the warpath again, and

Mordecai was again the target of his rage. In fact, the situation was so bad now, that Mordecai had left his post of duty and instead was in mourning—dressed in sackcloth, sitting cross-legged near the gate of the palace.

"Why is he mourning?" Esther demanded impatiently.

"Haven't you heard?" Hatach asked. "It's the new decree published by the king and his prime minister, Haman."

"What decree is that?"

Hatach continued, "A decree that all Jews shall be killed on a given date during the coming year. It's all here in this copy of the edict written by Haman and signed with the royal seal." He handed her a rolled-up parchment.

"Haman!" Esther almost screamed. "I should have known!" Her knees went weak as she slumped back onto her couch. Shocked, she knew exactly why all this was happening. A showdown was coming, and Mordecai was in the middle of it. It was obvious now that Haman hated Mordecai more than anyone else, and because of it, he was taking it out on every Jew in the kingdom of Persia.

And Esther's heart was pounding for another reason too. If all Jews were in danger now, then she was in danger too. She was a Jew. No one in the palace knew about that except Mordecai. No one—at least that's what she hoped.

Are there others now who know my secret? Does Haman know? she wondered. It did seem unlikely that she could have been in the palace this long with no one knowing of her background. Surely a young woman did not become queen without her private information becoming everyone's business sooner or later. Or so it would seem. When Esther thought of it that way, it made her head spin, her face flush, and her hands tremble.

CHAPTER 30

"Your Highness?" Hatach bent over Esther and cooled her forehead with a wet cloth. "Are you all right?" Taamina fanned her face, and Droxshana brought her a drink of water.

"I'm sorry the news upset you so much, Your Majesty. If I had known it would disturb you this much, I wouldn't have told you." Droxshana and the rest of Esther's maiden attendants had crowded around, and Hatach gave them all a worried glance. "Is Hegai here yet?" he asked. "Maybe he knows something about all this."

He turned his attention to Esther again. "Why does the news of such a decree disturb you, Your Highness, and who is this Mordecai that it should trouble you so?"

Esther eyes blurred again as she stared up at Hatach and the young women. *Shall I tell Hatach?* He was a faithful servant and a friend, but could she be sure he would keep her secret? She didn't know much about Haman's decree, but it sounded serious. *Will it make a difference if Hatach knows I am a Jewess? Can I trust him?* Esther just couldn't be sure.

She took a few sips of water but ignored Hatach's questions. "It bothers me that an officer of the king can make such a decree and has so much power to harm people." She stared at Hatach and then Droxshana. "Thanks to Haman, this decree is a disaster for Mordecai and his people! It's their death warrant!" She paused as if waiting for a reaction, but Hatach and Droxshana just stared at her dumbfounded.

"Someone must do something about it." Esther was really getting agitated. "What does Haman have against Jews, anyway?"

Hatach and Droxshana looked at each other in alarm.

"Well!"

"Well—I'm—not sure there's anything anyone can do about it!"

"What do you mean, you are 'not sure there's anything anyone can do about it'?" Esther was getting more and more upset and starting to wring her hands.

Just then Hegai arrived all out of breath. He took one look at Esther and knelt by her couch. "I came as quickly as I could, Your Highness. What is it?"

"Hatach tells me the prime minister has written a decree that all the Jews are soon to be executed. I wouldn't have even known about it if Hatach hadn't told me. And now Mordecai is in mourning, and it just shouldn't be that way! Mordecai was the one who reported the plot to assassinate the king!" Esther was near tears. "Can't someone do something to stop Haman?" Esther knew she needed to keep her emotions under control. Already she had said too much.

Hegai glanced at Hatach and then at Esther. "If it pleases the queen, may I speak freely?"

"Yes, of course."

Hegai glanced at the floor. "Unfortunately, when a royal decree is made and stamped with the king's own seal, the decree becomes a law, and it's final. It can't be revoked."

Esther looked surprised. "You mean, it can't be changed?"

Hegai heaved a sigh. "I'm afraid not."

"Can't the king change it? It's his seal."

Hegai shook his head. "That's not the way the laws work in Persia."

Esther got to her feet and went directly to her writing desk.

She picked up a quill and began to write a letter on a piece of parchment. The letter was short but direct.

"Hatach, take this letter to Mordecai now." She rolled up the parchment and sealed it. "And see that he's clothed with this robe." Esther handed Hatach a neatly folded robe of royal blue. "When he's read the message, tell him I would like a written response. I'll wait until you return with his answer.

"I can't believe King Xerxes knows this is happening!" she told Hegai after Hatach had left. "After all Mordecai has done to honor the king and save his life, why are he and his people being repaid this way?" Esther's eyes flashed. "Why would the king authorize the destruction of all the Jews in the first place? It just doesn't make sense! There's something else going on here!" Hegai was silent; it was plain he didn't know how to answer her.

"You're afraid of Haman!" Esther stated. "Well, I am too, but I think it's high time someone stood up to him!"

Within the hour, Hatach returned. Mordecai had refused to take the garment Esther sent. Hatach had found him dressed in the clothes of a mourner—sackcloth, dust, and ashes. Mordecai's response surprised her. "Why should I be clothed in fine raiment when God's people are in such danger?"

Esther guessed that Mordecai felt he was partly to blame for the crisis at hand, but as far as she was concerned, there was another part to the crisis as well. Haman was a spiteful, hateful, vengeful man. Mordecai was now fighting against impossible odds. No wonder he was mourning! If God was going to undo all the damage Haman had set in motion, maybe mourning and fasting was the only thing anybody could do.

And by now there was more news from the palace. As Esther listened to Hegai's explanation of recent events, the whole picture began to come together. Evidently, King Xerxes had asked his seven chief counselors what he could do to bring strength and peace to his entire kingdom, from Libya to Central Asia. Haman, one of the royal counselors, spoke of several recent uprisings in the empire. He claimed that the clan of people behind the attacks were hostile and warlike and could no longer be trusted to keep the laws of the land.

Haman assured the king that he didn't think it was wise to tolerate these people. It was his opinion that a decree should be written to destroy their entire race. If the world was rid of these people, peace and prosperity would no doubt come to the kingdom of Persia. The prime minister even offered to help pay for the enforcement of the decree—a whopping ten thousand talents of silver!

That Haman never mentioned the name of the hated race seemed to be an oversight, and it was never brought up. The king didn't ask, and Haman didn't tell. It was simply left as a technicality to be dealt with when the decree should be finally drawn up.

But there was more. Haman was very superstitious. Which day should the decree actually be issued, and which specific day of the year would be best to carry out the death sentence against the Jews? As was his custom, he consulted the best astrologers and soothsayers to determine which day to carry out each part of the plan. If Haman was to have success, everything must be perfect.

The astrologers Haman consulted with read the signs of the zodiac every day for a week preceding the day he made his proposal to the king. Chicken bones were studied, as well as pig's intestines, and the behavior of mice in a maze. Leaves were thrown into water and watched as to which way they would float. Palm readers were hired, lots were cast, the movement of clouds was measured, the flight of birds charted, and of course, the phases of the moon were checked for any luck they might bring Haman.

And so the thirteenth day of the month of Adar was chosen, a number that would most certainly bring bad luck with it for the

Jews. According to the oddsmakers among the court magicians and soothsayers, the number thirteen would guarantee the worst possible case of misfortune available to humankind.

By now, everyone who had read the decree knew that the destruction was to take place during the month of Adar. The king had even given Haman his own royal ring and seal to carry out this new edict. Haman was already the most powerful man in the kingdom next to Xerxes, and now with this seal of authority, he would be invincible. Any decree signed and sealed with this seal would be as final as if the king himself had issued it.

Esther felt sad as she listened to the details of the story. Haman's lies were outrageous! The Jews were not at all what he was making them out to be! That Haman had managed to spin such a tall tale made her angry. He was making trouble for her people, but he was also making King Xerxes look like a fool too. This was her husband they were talking about!

She was glad to hear one small detail, though. Hegai told her that King Xerxes had managed to do the right thing when Haman offered him the enormous bribe of ten thousand pieces of silver. He had turned it down. "At least Xerxes has some dignity. After all, he is the king," Hegai added. "He's the richest, most powerful man in the world. Why should he need the prime minister's silver?"

But it was small comfort to Esther when she thought about the fate of her people being in the hands of a wicked man like Haman. That an entire race of people could die in one day because of one selfish man's aspirations was a horrible nightmare.

And then there was the chilling reality that Esther herself was a Jew! What would become of her? Could she continue to keep her secret now that the decree had been announced, and, if so, for how much longer? Was it possible that Haman did, indeed, have inside information about her background?

CHAPTER 31

The next morning, royal scribes were summoned to the court to make copies of Haman's decree. Enough copies had to be made to send to the seven imperial princes, twenty royal satraps, and one hundred twenty-seven governors of provinces throughout the empire.

"The decree has to be written in the language and dialect of each country," Hatach told Esther. He read the words slowly from the scroll in his hands, glancing often at Esther. "The decree gives the order that local officials and citizens in every city are to attack and kill all Jews in one single day. Young and old will die together, including women and children; and those who destroy them may plunder their homes and businesses."

Esther was horrified as she listened to Hatach read the edict! She reminded herself that this decree could not be reversed. When a Persian law went into effect, it could not be repealed. Nothing she could do would change that. The king himself was powerless to change the decree, even if he wanted to.

She shuddered as she contemplated the future. *Shall I tell someone about my secret? Who can I trust enough to really do that? Hatach? Hegai? The king?* Telling the king seemed the right thing to do. After all, he was her husband. But something held her back. Perhaps the time wasn't yet right.

By noon royal couriers were already gathering in the courtyard of the citadel for last-minute instructions. They were to ride out late that afternoon in order to take advantage of the cool evening air. They would ride half the night, and then get a short rest before starting out again before dawn. When they rode through desolate areas, they were instructed to travel in groups. Those who must ride far would need to take provisions for the journey. As Esther watched through the harem palace gates, she could see Arabian steeds, sturdy mules, and camels being prepared for the journey. Some messengers would ride in chariots. The distance and terrain would determine the type of mount.

Tears welled up in Esther's eyes. Was there nothing she could do? She watched the couriers ride off in ten different directions, but she said nothing. Finally, she left the window and retired to pray in her inner chambers.

"Your Highness," Hatach said later that afternoon, as he appeared in the doorway of the receiving room. He bowed respectfully. "You've been invited to the king's personal quarters for a celebration."

Esther looked up from her seat on the couch. "A celebration? What is being celebrated?"

Hatach's gaze dropped to the floor. "A feast and a ceremonial toast to the success of the new decree."

The scroll Esther was reading dropped from her hands and rolled to the floor. She said nothing, but the pained expression on her face revealed her emotions.

"Am I to understand that you don't wish to attend?" he finally said.

Esther hesitated for several long moments, struggling over the decision. "No, I'll attend," she finally said, but her hesitation told Hatach the real story. The thought of going to such a dinner party turned her stomach. Haman had planned this awful, terrible tragedy for her people, and he was gloating over it! That he could hate an entire race of people was understandable. Not right, but understandable. It had been the nation of Israel that had destroyed his people, the Amalekites, centuries earlier; and now he was seeking the ultimate revenge with all the demonic powers that were within him. Human nature is like that.

But in her heart, Esther knew that the decree was more about Mordecai than anything else because Haman had never kept his hatred of Mordecai a secret.

Had the king known the whole story of Haman's treachery and his design to kill her people, he would have never agreed to such a decree. She was sure of that. And if she did finally get up the courage to tell the king that she was part of the hated race, too, it was hard to guess how he would react. If she told him the truth about Haman's plot, would he be angry at Haman? He would have to be, it seemed. She couldn't imagine it turning out any other way.

And then another thought struck her. When the plot against her people was uncovered, would the king be angry at her for not warning him she was in trouble? Would he be furious that she had not told him she was a Jew? Or did any of this matter at all? No matter what the king's reaction might be, he was not going to be able to stop the death decree against her people now scheduled for the thirteenth day in the month of Adar.

Esther swallowed hard as she contemplated her life. Living in the palace often left her feeling incredibly lonely. On the day she had been taken from home to compete in the beauty contest, she had known she would be all alone and that things would never again be the same.

The ties with her family and the Jewish community had been cut. They were all she had ever known, and now they were gone. She had copies of the Torah in her private quarters, so she could read, but it wasn't the same as having people of her faith to worship with and eat and celebrate together on the Jewish feast days! And she no longer had opportunities to attend the Sabbath services. A Persian queen couldn't freely leave the palace compound and mix with common people. It just wasn't done. And even if it were, attending Sabbath services would reveal her secret.

As Esther prepared for bed that night, her heart was heavy with fear. Parvona spent extra time brushing Esther's hair, and Morvari prepared a warm bath with perfumed oils to help her relax, but nothing seemed to work. She just couldn't escape the sense of dread that loomed on the horizon.

Haman's new law had become the greatest crisis of her life. Her people were going to die if something wasn't done to save them, but she couldn't imagine what that something might be. She wasn't sure that she herself would escape, and that made her burden even greater to bear.

So much was happening so fast, and there seemed to be no one she could turn to for advice or comfort.

CHAPTER 32

Esther wished with all her heart that she had just one good friend she could confide in. Someone she could tell about this horrible nightmare that had become part of her life. She wondered if any of her attending maidens would understand or could be trusted with such a secret.

And then she thought of Droxshana. She was the one attendant Esther felt she could really confide in. If Esther had a best friend in the palace, someone she could count on, Droxshana would be that person. Now Esther asked herself whether Droxshana might be the one she could tell the deepest and most hidden parts of her life. At this moment, there seemed no one else but her.

While her maidens prepared her for bed, Esther prayed as she had never prayed before. "Please, Lord, don't leave me all alone during this crisis! Give me someone I can trust. Help me to know if I can trust Droxshana!"

In the end, Esther asked Droxshana to stay, and they talked late into the night. She told of the horrors of being orphaned by a plague. She told Droxshana of her loving cousin Mordecai, who had taken her in and adopted her as his own. Droxshana heard of Esther's Jewish roots and the secret she had kept hidden all these months.

And as they talked of Haman's decree that now threatened to

sweep away an entire race of people, Droxshana's eyes filled with tears. "Why didn't you tell me about this before?" she cried, as she hugged Esther close. "You should have known I would understand! You should have known your secret would be safe with me." Then Droxshana suddenly grew stern. "I would rather suffer with you than to allow my queen to go through this alone!"

"Thank you!" Esther smiled through her own tears. "You're such a dear friend, and you're right! I should have trusted you long ago with all of this, but my cousin Mordecai warned me not to trust anyone with my secret."

"But he didn't know me," Droxshana protested and gave Esther another hug.

Esther closed her eyes and sighed with relief. "You'll never know how much this means to me, Droxshana. In spite of the dangers that seem to surround me, I know I need to be brave, and I realize that you are the one friend to help me do that."

The next morning, Hatach brought Esther word that Mordecai was still walking the streets of Susa, wailing loudly and bitterly and tearing his clothes. "He's been allowed time off from his job in the palace because he's in mourning," Hatach told Esther.

It broke Esther's heart to think of Cousin Mordecai in such a state of mind. She had heard by now that her people all over the empire were mourning the coming catastrophe. But what could she do? She reviewed her limitations. *The decree has become Persian law, and Persian laws can't be changed. And I can't approach the king without an invitation.* Persian laws said that unless invited, women were not allowed in the royal court—not even the queen! If she requested an audience with the king, he might fly into a rage and order her execution. His quick temper was well-known.

What to do? By nightfall, Esther was beside herself with anxiety. When she finally did lie down for the night, she slept fitfully. All night she tossed and turned, trying to come up with a plan that might alter the destiny of hundreds of thousands of Jews! But by dawn, she was no closer to a solution.

She rose to a new day, but didn't have the appetite to eat. And then about midmorning, another written message from Cousin Mordecai was delivered. It contained a frightening suggestion: "My dear Esther, I'm sure by now you know what you must do. The king is evidently unaware of Haman's real intention, and you must make it known to him. There is no one better suited than you to give the king the information. Go. And may the God of our fathers strengthen you and give you courage in this step of faith."

Esther wondered at Mordecai's daring suggestion. Was it possible he had forgotten the penalty for such an act? Working in the royal court as he did, she could hardly believe he would suggest going uninvited to see the king—and she wrote Mordecai immediately telling him so.

By now the messages between Mordecai and Esther were becoming more and more frequent, and she wondered that Hatach hadn't discovered how she and Mordecai were connected. Or maybe he did know. Perhaps he was just keeping it quiet and doing everything in his power to help her.

She sent the return message with Hatach, instructing the chamberlain to once again wait for a reply. "No one is allowed to go to the citadel without an invitation," her message read. "I would probably be killed. Even if I am the queen, and even if the king does love me, he would never allow such disregard for the rules of the royal court. Look how he treated Vashti. The only exception would be if the king would hold out his golden scepter to accept my visit to his court. It's been thirty days since I visited him last, and there's no guarantee that he would be pleased to see me."

But Mordecai was not silenced by Esther's excuses. "Do you

think that you yourself will escape?" came his ready reply in the next message. "Though you are in the king's house and the queen of his royal harem, Haman's law will exclude no favorites! You can be sure that no more mercy will be shown you than is extended to all the other Jews! If you don't speak now, then God will have to deliver His people another way. If that happens, then you most certainly will be destroyed. Can you really afford to run that risk, Esther? Can you afford to have that on your conscience?"

And then the tone of Mordecai's message softened as he called her by her Jewish name. "Who knows, Hadassah? God may have called you to the kingdom for just such a time as this."

CHAPTER 33

"What shall I do, Shan?" Esther asked her best friend. It was late afternoon again, and the faint clinking of plates told Esther it wouldn't be long until the evening meal.

"I think you should do as your cousin Mordecai has suggested." Droxshana's expression was earnest. "Is there any other way?"

"You think I should go to the king? Without being invited?" Esther's expression showed her surprise.

"This is a terrible time for you and your people. Can you imagine a better time to take the risk?"

"But—but, what if the king doesn't hold out his scepter to me? I could be executed!"

"You could." Droxshana replied matter-of-factly. "And if you don't speak out, in the end, you'll be executed anyway!"

"I guess you are right," Esther admitted. "That's exactly what my cousin Mordecai said, but before today I didn't want to face that possibility."

"Tell me more about your people." Droxshana settled down among the cushions in Esther's reading room. "Tell me the history of the Jews and how it came to be that the Jews came to live in Persia." It was amazing to see Droxshana show such interest in Jewish history. Esther would never have imagined that a Persian girl would be interested in the past history of her people. After all, the Persian Empire stretched from Libya to Central Asia.

What importance did the history of Israel and the Jewish people have for a girl from the greatest empire the world had ever known?

For several hours, they sat in a corner of the room while Esther recounted stories of Abraham, Isaac, and Jacob. She told the tale of Israel's slavery and deliverance from Egypt, of their wanderings in the desert, and the conquest of Canaan. She told of how the judges ruled the land, but that the twelve tribes wanted to be like the nations around them and have their own king. Droxshana was truly entertained as she heard stories of Samuel, David, and Solomon. She grew sad as she heard the tales of how king after king led the people into apostasy, idol worship, and even child sacrifice. And, of course, Esther told her the saddest story of all, that Jehovah had finally allowed Babylon to conquer and carry her people off into slavery.

The regular time for the evening meal came and went, and still Esther talked on. It was as if she needed to hear the history of her people once again just to remind herself of how wonderful it had been to be part of God's chosen people.

What amazed Droxshana the most about the stories was Jehovah being Israel's one and only God—an invisible God. When the Jews lived up to their covenant with Him, He could and would deliver the people from their enemies. Time and time again, He had done so. Jehovah had never stopped loving the Jews as His people, and one day soon, He would send the Messiah to save them from their sins.

"An invisible God?" Droxshana grew thoughtful at the idea of a God that couldn't be seen. "An invisible God who blesses those who serve Him and obey Him? That's a strange idea, but I think I like it."

Esther gazed at her friend gratefully. "Thank you for listening, Droxshana. It makes it easier for me to decide what I need to do.

I still have to make a decision, but I feel stronger now that I've talked with you." Esther's eyes betrayed the fear she still felt.

"Your Highness," Droxshana bowed her head, "if it pleases the queen, I would remind you of all you have told me here this afternoon. Many, many times Jehovah has delivered your people from your enemies. He has never stopped loving your people, even though you live in a foreign land. Do you think His love for you is any different today from what it has ever been?"

"You make it sound so easy," Esther admitted.

"Not easy, Your Highness. Just clear. You know what you must do. I think you're just trying to find the courage to do it."

Esther nodded her head, but remained quiet.

"And remember, you said your God rewards obedience. You wouldn't want to be found working against Jehovah, would you?"

Droxshana's advice seemed to clarify Esther's duty. How could she do anything but confront the king on the reasons behind Haman's decree? She could and she would, but how to do it was the issue now. How could she tell King Xerxes of Haman's plot, when the king had so much confidence in Haman? The prime minister was his right-hand man. The king was convinced that his empire was safer and more prosperous with Haman around.

But she needed to tell the king just the same. Before she lay down to rest for the night, Esther sat down at her desk and wrote out another message to Cousin Mordecai. "Gather together all the Jews who are in Susa," she requested. "Pray and fast for me, and I and my attending maidens will do the same. After three days, I'll go to the king, even though it's against the law. And if I perish, I perish." The message was simple but to the point. Esther now knew that it was her duty; there was no other way. God was calling her to do a special job for Him, and she knew she had to obey.

And Mordecai did as Esther asked. All-night prayer sessions were held from one end of Susa to the other, wherever Jews gathered together to call on the Lord. Mordecai even sent couriers to groups of Jews in distant cities such as Persepolis and Ecbatana.

Esther prayed and fasted with her maidens too. The queen drank water and fruit nectars, but she didn't eat at all. And as her earnest words of prayer rose to heaven, the maiden attendants all wondered at her faith.

"How can you be so calm?" Ovoga asked, her deep dark eyes searching Esther's face.

"I guess it comes from believing the words of the Lord my God. Jehovah has promised that He'll never leave me or forsake me."

"But we can't even see your God. How can you speak to Him as if He's right here?"

"I believe He is here," Esther said. "He's everywhere."

Taamina's eyes sparkled with earnest excitement. "Will you teach us more about Jehovah? The only gods we've ever worshiped are gods that are cruel and that demand pain and suffering."

And that's how Esther came to lead the most important prayer session of her young life. Three days of intense prayer and fasting left her feeling famished, but refreshed and hopeful. As the hours flew by, more and more she felt warmed and comforted by the Spirit of God.

On the morning of the third day, Esther gathered her maidens together and prayed with them one last time before setting out for the palace. She trembled as she realized the big moment had come, but she wasn't sure whether it was nerves or lack of food.

In order to find just the right look for Esther, the girls dressed their queen in gown after gown. They tried a scarlet colored garment and then a powder blue one, but nothing seemed just right. Finally, they selected a white gown of silk that gave Esther a look of innocence and simplicity. Then they sprayed on the sweetest smelling spikenard from her stock of perfumes.

"Do you think the king will find me attractive? It's important that I look just right," Esther fussed. "He needs to like what he sees even from a distance, in case I never get close enough for him to smell the spikenard I'm wearing."

The girls wanted to laugh when she put it that way, but they knew this was no time to be making jokes.

Esther tried to put them at ease, reminding her attendants that none of them had to go with her if they were afraid. "This is my problem, not yours," she said.

"That's not true." Droxshana moved closer to Esther. "Where you go, we will go." But they all knew what the outcome of this daring venture might be. King Xerxes had been known to execute people on a whim and then later tell his court that he regretted having done so.

When Esther was finally ready to leave, Hatach led the way down the pathways to the great hall of the citadel palace. Harbona had told Hatach the king was now sitting in court. The question was, Would he welcome Esther into his presence with his scepter or reject her and give her the death penalty?

CHAPTER 34

When Esther and her entourage of maidens arrived at the massive bronze gates of the citadel, the guards bowed respectfully. It seemed like a dream as they entered the palace courtyard. With a prayer on her lips, Esther glided from corridor to portico to the inner court of the palace, across polished floors of red and blue and black marble.

As they neared the open antechamber just off the royal court, Esther could see the tall doors of ebony gilded in ivory and gold. This was a different reception chamber from the one Esther had visited before. Here King Xerxes received all royal visitors and heard all cases that concerned his government abroad. Right now he was seated, facing the open doorways to the great room, listening to arguments being brought before him. She watched the king's eyes as the voice of a courtier droned on and on with the details of the case. He looked bored, but it took her breath away to see him so strikingly handsome, with his hair and beard braided up in the usual style of royalty. The king's right elbow was on the elaborate armrest of his throne, his chin in his hand.

And then his eye strayed momentarily, and he caught sight of the beautiful Esther standing patiently in the outer court. In that instant, time once again stood still for the young queen. During the previous days, she had spent many an hour contemplating this exact moment. Would the king be angry that she had come to the court uninvited? Or would he welcome her and hold out his scepter?

Instantly, King Xerxes' eyes brightened, and he sat up a little straighter. His eyes were on Esther as he held up his hand to the speaker for silence and stretched his golden scepter toward her.

That was the signal she had been waiting for. This was the moment she had both dreaded and hoped for. Esther stepped slowly forward, leaving her attending maidens behind. An enormous hush fell over the place as Esther entered the lavish throne room filled with royal courtiers and counselors. She seemed to glide as she approached the king on his throne and the out-stretched scepter.

When she finally stood directly in front of the enormous throne, she dropped to her knees and reached out to touch the very tip of his jeweled scepter.

"To what do I owe this visit by the most beautiful woman in the kingdom?" he asked graciously. "Ask anything and I will give it to you, even up to half my kingdom."

Of course, he didn't literally mean what he said. "Half of his kingdom" was just an expression that showed appreciation of the person he was greeting, and she knew that now was the time to take advantage of the king's good mood.

"Please, Your Majesty, if I and my maidens have found favor in your eyes, accept a royal invitation for you and Prince Haman to dine with me." Esther looked calm, but inside she was trembling. "Please come to my palace quarters," she added, "to dine with me this evening at a special banquet I have planned for you."

With a nod and a smile for the beautiful young woman who had captured his heart, the king responded, "Your wish is my command!"

If he could have seen the disapproving looks on the faces of the royal counselors standing behind him, the king might have been surprised. Many in his court were becoming increasingly critical of his growing attachment to this fair young lady. She was his new queen, but was she growing too powerful for the king's own good? Would she become another Vashti, daring to break from tradition and inevitably cause the royal court more embarrassment? It irritated them that King Xerxes hadn't hesitated in the slightest about Esther coming to the throne room uninvited. A woman was not to do that! Not even the queen! Vashti had never dared do it, and her refusal to come on the night of the great banquet had cost her the position as Xerxes' queen. Was Esther gaining more power already than Vashti had ever had?

Esther could see the unhappy faces of the king's counselors, but she ignored their cold stares as she heard the king command, "Send for Haman and give him the invitation!" He turned his attention again to Esther. "Haman and I would be glad to accept your invitation," he said graciously.

The next few hours flew by as Esther prepared for the evening she knew must count for everything. The harem director, chamberlains, and maiden attendants all helped out. Nothing could be overlooked. Nothing must be left to chance in the preparations for this extraordinary evening with its very special guests.

But the hour finally arrived, and Esther knew she had never been so nervous in her life. Not even her very first encounter with the king had been this charged with electricity and emotion.

The sun was just beginning to set as the king and his prime minister arrived at the receiving room of Esther's royal suite where the banquet would be held. The king's reclining couch was placed in the very center of the large room, with Haman's couch on one side and Esther's on the other. The king's couch was elaborate, made of pure gold, with legs carved as lions' feet and dragons arching over its gilded backrest. Blue and purple silk covered its plush cushions. Haman's couch was made of ebony and ivory, with cushions of red, and Esther's was a smaller silver couch with white cushions.

The evening's meal wasn't a full-course banquet, but only a splendid array of appetizers and desserts. The delicious-looking food was spread out before King Xerxes and Haman on platters of silver, gold, and mother-of-pearl. Esther's attendants served the usual pastries, tiny layered cakes, and tarts they knew the king liked. They also served a variety of olives, cheeses, crackers, and fruits of all kinds. Dariush, the king's royal taster, also attended. He accompanied the king everywhere, along with the king's two private chamberlains.

Hatach advised Esther to offer the king's favorite wines, and she reluctantly agreed. She wished she didn't have to serve the wine. She knew how easily things could get out of hand when the king and his guests began drinking, and she knew she couldn't afford to let that happen. She needed the king to be in a good mood when she told him that his prime minister was plotting her death and the total annihilation of her people!

If the king drank too much wine, he might not believe her claim. She also realized that he and the prime minister were very good friends. How could she say what she needed to say without making it sound ludicrous? Though she was the king's wife and the queen, she was just a woman—and a very young woman at that. She had beauty and charm on her side, but right now it seemed that this was all she had. She was afraid that even these things could easily be taken from her when the secret got out that she was a Jew.

And then what she feared might happen was exactly what took place. As the servants brought out course after course of the delightful treats, there just seemed no ideal moment for her to open her heart to the king. Meanwhile, the two men were drinking more and more of the wines. Finally, the king turned to Esther and asked her reason for inviting the two men to the meal. Banquets were planned for a purpose, and the king suspected she had her reasons for this one.

"What is your pleasure?" his voice slurred slightly from the effects of the wine. "Speak now, and it will be given you—even up to half the kingdom." Once again, the king made his ceremonial offer, but Esther knew King Xerxes was too drunk to think clearly. The moment had passed, and she knew the opportunity to speak her mind was gone.

"May my king live forever!" She lowered her gaze and bowed her head. "If it is pleasing to the king, I request that you and Haman come again tomorrow evening for another feast in the king's honor." Her head remained down until she heard his voice.

To Esther's relief, the king agreed to a repeat invitation. Maybe he realized that he was too drunk to stay longer. Maybe he felt he was embarrassing Esther and just needed to go before he made a fool of himself.

CHAPTER 35

The night was still young when Haman and King Xerxes left Esther's suite, their attendants following. The king was escorted to the citadel, and Haman was taken out through the main palace gate. Several officials were still there on duty, including Mordecai, who had returned to his post as royal scribe.

It was obvious he was drunk as he wobbled through this main gate. Several officials who were talking there quickly knelt on the stone pavement with their faces to the floor. Haman nodded with satisfaction at the men but then noticed Mordecai standing to one side, a moist clay tablet still in his hand. Mordecai bowed in quiet respect, but didn't kneel on the floor with the other men.

Haman was furious! "You foolish Jew!" he slurred in a rage. "Don't you know that I hold your life in my hands? The king's decree says that all Jews are to be destroyed in the month of Adar! Bow the knee before me, you Jewish dog. I demand your respect and your worship!" It was clear that Haman hated Mordecai now more than ever, but Mordecai remained quiet, not even flinching in the face of Haman's outburst.

The prime minister spat on the floor in Mordecai's direction. "If every Jew is as big a fool as you, then you all deserve to die!" Haman's hand shook as he jabbed an accusing finger at Mordecai. "How you ever managed to get a position as scribe at the gate of the royal court, I'll never know, but I can't wait until the day they drag you away to your execution, and I'm going to see to it personally!"

The prime minister staggered off, his attendants and body-guards following close behind. Several of them glared at Mordecai, muttering curse words at him and promising him they would have their revenge.

Early the next morning, Hatach brought Esther word that the king hadn't slept well and had been up half the night. Esther was immediately alarmed. "Do you think it was because of something he ate last night—something we served him?" Would the king think she had fed him something poisonous? She could not imagine what might have made him sick. She trusted every one of the servants in her kitchens and all her attending maidens. She trusted them with her own life, and certainly with the life of the king.

Hatach shook his head. "I don't know what caused the king's insomnia, but Harbona, his chamberlain, said that when the king couldn't sleep, he called in his scribes to read from the records in the royal archives. And while they were reading, they came across the story of how Bigthan and Teresh had plotted to assassinate the king. While they were reading, they discovered something. Nothing had been done to reward the ones who were responsible for uncovering the plot against the king."

"Still not rewarded?" Esther asked.

"That's right!" Hatach's face grew serious. "People who uncover such plots usually receive a reward, but this time it didn't happen. Perhaps the king did ask someone to reward Mordecai, but no one actually carried out the order. Or perhaps someone in the palace didn't want Mordecai to get that reward or recognition. Anyway," Hatach continued, "you'll never guess what's going on at the palace right now. After reading the account in the royal records, the king is trying to plan a good way to reward Mordecai."

"Right now?"

"That's right, and from what I understand, Haman is in the king's receiving room, talking with the king about how to reward 'the man whom the king wishes to honor.'" Hatach spoke in a boring monotone, imitating one of the royal courtiers, but there was a twinkle in his eye.

"Haman?" Esther looked surprised, ignoring the humor of the moment. "Well, at least the man is doing something worthwhile with his time."

"Your Highness," Hatach stated carefully. "I don't believe you fully understand what's happening here."

Esther looked confused.

"Your Highness, Haman hates Mordecai." Hatach had to smile to himself. *Esther is beautiful, indeed, but inexperienced and naive.* "You always do hope for the best in everyone, don't you?" He sighed.

"I know they're enemies, Hatach," Esther responded. "Mordecai is like poison to the man."

"Yes, Your Highness, but my question is an obvious one, I think. Whom do you think the king is going to reward?"

"That would be Mordecai. And perhaps, the slave boy in the kitchen. What was his name?"

Hatach shook his head. "I can't say I know."

Esther continued, "Well, I hope the king follows through with this. If ever anyone deserved such a reward, it would be Mordecai. He's always got the best of everyone at heart, and he never expects anything in return!"

"Well then, you're going to love the irony." Hatach winked. "Harbona overhead the king asking for Haman's opinion on what type of reward should be given to one whom the king delights to honor. Based on the official records the king was reading last night and his desire to reward the ones who uncovered the assassination plot, I think it's safe to say that—"

Esther suddenly interrupted Hatach. "Wait a minute! Are you telling me that the king is getting ready to reward Mordecai, but Haman doesn't know that's who the king is talking about?" Esther was smiling with delight now at the turn of events. "Oh my! I can't wait to see how this turns out."

CHAPTER 36

Later that afternoon, Droxshana and Esther were in the queen's private suite, talking about the day's events. Esther had spent the late hours of the morning in one of her favorite pastimes—reading. Spread out around her were a wide range of parchment scrolls and clay tablets brought in from the royal archives.

"Look at this," Esther said, holding up a clay tablet. "It's all here." Her eyes scanned the cuneiform writing on the hardened red clay. " 'And it came to pass that Bigthan and Teresh, two of the king's officers who guarded the doorway to the king's own living quarters, became angry and conspired to assassinate King Xerxes. But Mordecai, royal scribe in the gate of the king, found out about the plot and told Queen Esther, who in turn reported it to the king, giving credit to Mordecai. And when the report was investigated and found to be true, the two officials were executed by being impaled.' "

"See." Esther pointed to the clay tablet. "The entire story was recorded in the book of the royal annals in the presence of the king."

As she was talking, she kept glancing toward the open window. A commotion could be heard approaching in the street just outside the palace gate. She glanced at Droxshana. "Do you know what's going on out there?"

At that moment, Taamina, one of the other maidens, went

rushing by. Droxshana grabbed the sleeve of Taamina's tunic. "What's the commotion in the street all about?" she asked.

"It's a big parade!" Taamina's face was flushed. "The prime minister is walking down the street leading a horse. And you won't believe who's riding the horse! It's Mordecai!" Her eyes were fairly dancing. "Come and see!"

Esther and Droxshana hurried to a window overlooking the courtyard. Beyond that they could see the street that ran past the palace grounds. A huge crowd lined the street, making it impossible for the two women to see anything. Finally, Esther called to Hatach and asked if he could clear the people away from the side of the street next to the palace grounds.

It took a bit of time, but palace guards finally managed to do it, and then Esther could clearly see a horse coming. The horse was all decked out in the trappings of a royal steed, and Mordecai was astride the horse. His garment was covered with ten thousand tiny diamonds that flashed white and blue and green in the afternoon sun.

Mordecai was also wearing a crown, and as the procession drew nearer the gate, Esther gasped. The crown had to be one from the king's treasury. No one would dare to wear such a crown unless he was connected to royalty. It had to be one of King Xerxes' crowns, no doubt seized as booty from some enemy king in a military campaign. And walking along in front of the horse and Mordecai was Haman, calling out like a town crier at the top of his voice, "This is what the king does for those he wishes to honor!"

"Can you believe it?" Hatach stepped up beside Esther. "And this from a man who would rather play with scorpions than be in the same room with Mordecai!"

Esther stood on her tiptoes to get a better view. "It must be humiliating for Haman, having to lead the horse on foot. He looks like a stable hand, while Mordecai gets to ride the horse like a king." She turned to Hatach. "I wonder how much that royal robe is worth."

"I could guess," Hatach replied. "I once saw King Xerxes wear one like it for a holiday parade, and they said it was worth at least seventy-five talents of gold. So I guess you're right. This must be a really embarrassing day for Haman. And, of course, a very satisfying day for Mordecai." Hatach turned to Esther. "Would you like to know the rest of the story?"

"The rest of the story?" Then Esther gave Hatach one of her sweet smiles. "Of course I would! But I have to say, after seeing all this, I don't think anything would surprise me."

"OK, let's see." Hatach gave Esther another wink. "It's true, Haman had no idea what was coming. He hadn't a clue when he walked into the king's breakfast chamber this morning that the king was about to honor Mordecai for helping to uncover the assassination plot. Probably all Haman was thinking about was that he had been honored by the invitation to dine with you and the king. He had already been promoted to the position of prime minister and had received permission to send out a decree to have Mordecai and his people destroyed. That was quite an accomplishment to be sure! And then first thing this morning, the king asks him a simple question—what should be done for the man the king delights to honor?" Hatach began to chuckle.

"Well, of course, Haman thought that the praise was due him and that the king certainly had him in mind for all the honors to come. So he made a fantastic proposal, and what you just saw is the result—the king's finest holiday apparel, a royal crown second only to the one King Xerxes himself wears, a purebred steed from a bloodline of horses the king's grandfather raised in the stables of Babylon, and of course, an important government official to lead the horse."

Hatach began to laugh again. "The king has no idea how much

Haman hates Mordecai, so the king's final command to Haman must have been excruciating—'Go do all this as you have suggested. Do it for the hero, Mordecai, and you yourself may personally lead the horse.'"

The royal parade was passing right in front of the palace gate now. Esther, Droxshana, and Hatach watched as the crowd cheered for Mordecai. Esther couldn't see Haman's face any longer, but by the way his shoulders slumped, she was sure there was going to be real trouble for all the shame Haman had to bear.

Almost in answer to her thoughts, Hatach added, "But that's still not the entire story, Your Highness."

"What else?" Esther asked.

"This morning in the royal kitchen, everybody was talking about how angry Haman was when he went home last night."

"Angry? I thought he looked pretty happy when he left the banquet."

"Well, maybe he was, but by the time he got home, they said he was really angry! Harbona told me that on the way home after the banquet, Haman met up with Mordecai, and Mordecai bowed but refused to kneel. He refused to kiss Haman's hand or to kneel with his face to the floor."

Esther shook her head in dismay. "No wonder Haman returned home angry!"

Hatach smiled again. "Anyway, the guards who escorted him home said he was shouting and cursing that he was going to kill Mordecai. And then this morning, we heard loud hammering near Haman's house, and everybody up that way says Haman has built a set of gallows. Really tall ones."

"Gallows!" Esther's face paled. "Haman is the second most powerful man in all of Persia. I guess he can do whatever he wants." She swallowed hard as she thought of who Haman would want to put on the gallows first. Everybody but the king, it seemed, knew the answer to that question. Even the beggars in the streets of Susa would say, "Mordecai."

By now Mordecai's parade had disappeared down the street. But Esther knew the parade wouldn't end the situation. If King Xerxes had humiliated Haman by forcing him to honor Mordecai publicly, then Haman would find a way to get back. He always did, and it wouldn't be the king who paid the price.

It didn't seem possible that Haman could order Mordecai's execution when the king had just given him the highest honors in the land, but with Haman in charge, she guessed anything was possible. And besides, Mordecai was a Jew. Haman had managed to get a law passed arranging for the destruction of an entire culture of people, and that meant Mordecai too.

CHAPTER 37

It was nearly time for the second evening banquet at Esther's suite. Droxshana had spent the afternoon helping Esther prepare for it, and it was a good thing. Esther knew this was probably the most important night of her life yet. What would happen when the king and Haman arrived for the second evening in a row? Would she have the courage to tell the king about Haman's plot to destroy her and her people? Would Haman find a way to talk his way out of this mess he was in? Would the king favor Esther or Haman? The answer to these questions seemed obvious to Esther, but then she thought of Vashti. As charming and beautiful as Vashti had been, she had still lost her position as queen.

Esther's worry and tension finally lead to a bad headache. Droxshana had to call in the doctor for the harem. The bald-headed man examined her and then prescribed a dose of artemisia and willow oil. Fortunately, the headache soon disappeared.

And then it was time for the king and Haman to arrive. When the guards escorted the two men to Esther's suite, the place looked and smelled heavenly. Fragrant flowers of pink, yellow, and rose were everywhere, and royal musicians had been called in to give the evening just the right ambiance. An ensemble of flutes, lyres, and dulcimers promised to make the evening a relaxing one, and the food was delightful as usual. The royal chef had worked all day making a variety of treats for the two distinguished guests.

Esther tried not to repeat the previous evening's menu and yet still offer the men some of their favorites.

But one thing would be different this evening. Esther had lost her opportunity the evening before when the men became too drunk to reason clearly. This evening she wouldn't make that same mistake. She would make her petition known as soon as appropriate, and if things went well, the drinking wouldn't get out of hand.

Haman made a big show with his arrival, but he was definitely not the same man he had been the evening before. Esther guessed that having to escort Mordecai's parade through the streets that afternoon hadn't made his day a good one at all.

But the king seemed to be in a good enough mood for all three of them. Esther couldn't bring herself to look the king in the eye. She was sure her fears were affecting her behavior, but she hoped it didn't show too much. Fortunately, her shy ways and long eyelashes seemed to have the desired effect on him.

When they were all comfortably seated on their reclining couches, the drinks and delicacies were served immediately. The king did not guess that Esther was about to make the announcement of her life, and Haman was doing his best to carry on a pleasant conversation with the king. Finally, however, Xerxes turned to her, and by the look on his face, she knew the moment had arrived.

His eyes were soft and a smile crinkled the corners of his mouth. "Tell me, my fair queen, what is it you desire of me? What is your request? You look stunning tonight, as usual. You've prepared an impressive evening for us. The food is sumptuous, and the surroundings are indeed pleasant. What is in your heart?" He smiled almost boyishly. "Just say the word, and it will be given you, even if it's up to half my kingdom."

"Thank you, my king." She smiled at his gracious words and

glanced around the room. Everything was just right—the musicians, the attentive servants, the flowers, the glowing lamps, the delicious food and wine. Esther was glad to see that King Xerxes was drinking sparingly of the wine. Maybe he regretted embarrassing her the evening before and was trying to make up for it. But she also knew that now was the time to speak. The moment had arrived!

Esther took a deep breath and sent a prayer to the God of her fathers. She would say what she needed to say because Mordecai had asked her to and because her people needed her to say it. Come what may, when this was over, no one would be able to say that Queen Esther had not done her part.

"May my lord, the king, live forever," she continued respectfully. "If I have found favor with you, O king, and if it pleases you, Your Majesty, my petition is that you grant me my life!" She paused long enough to let her words sink in, but not long enough to lose her train of thought. "My request is that you spare me and my people, for we have been sold for destruction, slaughter, and annihilation. If we had merely been sold as male and female slaves, I would have kept quiet, because such a thing would not justify disturbing the king."

King Xerxes was stunned. For the longest moment, he could only stare at Queen Esther, but then he finally found his voice. "Grant you your life? What are you talking about, Esther? And what people are you speaking of?"

"I'm a Jewess," Esther said the words slowly and deliberately.

"A Jewess!" the king shook his head as though he were in a dream. "You're a Jewess?"

Esther bowed her head humbly and waited but said nothing more.

"A Jewess!" the king repeated the words, not really understanding what they meant, and then his eyes narrowed. "Why are the Jews to be slaughtered? Who has planned such a thing? Who is responsible for this—this slavery and death you're talking about?"

Esther opened her mouth, but it seemed that her tongue was stuck. She wanted to get down off the couch and fall on her knees. She wanted to fall on her face in respect to the king, but she just sat motionless on her couch of silver and silk, not knowing what else to do.

"Who is this man?" the king repeated. His voice was angry now, and his fists went white around the knuckles. "Where is this villain who would dare do such a thing to my queen and her people?" It seemed that such a question could have no answer, that no man on earth would have been stupid enough to devise such a plan.

Esther slowly raised her hand and pointed at Haman, who was sitting opposite her, her voice trembling. "The adversary and enemy I speak of is this vile Haman!"

CHAPTER 38

And now Haman looked terrified! It was obvious that Esther's words were unexpected. He turned to the king first, and then to Esther. It was clear he wanted to say something, but he could only stammer out his shock. "I—I—I don't—understand!" It was amazing to see the usually suave Haman at a loss for words.

The king glared at Haman. "What have you done?"

And then Haman finally did find his voice, but the fear on his face was unmistakable. "You accuse me of trying to take the life of the queen? This isn't possible! There's been a terrible misunderstanding!"

"There certainly has!" the king shouted, his shock and anger evident. He stood to his feet, towering over Haman, who still reclined on his couch. The man he had chosen to promote above every other official in his kingdom was plotting to kill the queen.

King Xerxes stood there, clenching and unclenching his fists. Esther watched the expression on her husband's face as he finally stalked out of the room and into the garden courtyard to think. She could tell that his next move was going to be severe!

And now the terrified Haman suddenly flew into action. He jumped up from his couch and hurried to where Esther still reclined on her couch. "Please, Your Highness," he begged. "I'm innocent of such charges. I would never plot to take your life!"

Esther stared at the prime minister, trying to hold her emotions in check. "But you have plotted to take the life of my family and my people." There was no pity in her heart for this cruel man. No sympathy, but neither did she want to be cold and hateful. It was not the way Cousin Mordecai had raised her, and it was certainly not appropriate for a person of her standing.

"No! No! I would never have done such a thing!" Haman was getting desperate. "If—if I had known you were one of them, I—I would—!" He stopped short and suddenly fell to his knees beside Esther's couch. "I don't know what to say, Your Highness. Please, I beg of you, help me!"

Esther couldn't believe her ears! "After the horrible scheme you've plotted to destroy my people, you ask me to help you? And that's saying nothing about the dreadful way you've treated my cousin Mordecai!"

"Mordecai?" Haman's jaw fell even further. "Mordecai is your cousin?" At this news, Haman began to panic. He leaned over Esther's couch and clutched at her silken robe, making her pull back in anger and disgust!

On his knees before Esther was one of the cruelest and most treacherous men in all of Persia! Here was a man who would never show a mina's worth of mercy to anyone who didn't serve his purpose! The mean and spiteful man was now on his knees begging for mercy! But it was in vain because the very next event in this episode sealed Haman's fate completely.

At that very moment, the king returned to the banquet chamber. The stunned king saw Haman leaning over Esther's couch, clutching the queen's beautiful robe, screaming at her.

"Will my prime minister attack the queen even in my presence?" the king roared, pointing his finer at the frightened Haman.

Palace guards rushed forward and yanked Haman to his feet. Rustam, captain of the king's guard, pulled a black cloak from the shoulders of a guard standing nearby and threw it over Haman's head.

Everything was happening so fast, and there was confusion everywhere. Haman was screaming for mercy, the king was shaking his fist angrily, and Esther's maidens were pulling her away to one side of the room.

"Look, Your Majesty!" Harbona pointed out the window of the queen's banquet chamber. "There's the gallows Haman built to execute Mordecai, the scribe who uncovered the plot to assassinate you!"

Everyone turned to the window. Sure enough, through the open window of the banquet chamber, at some distance from the palace complex, they could see Haman's gallows. The structure was clearly silhouetted against the western horizon, still glowing pink and rose in the evening twilight. Earlier that day, Esther had heard the rumors about the amazing height of the gallows built to execute her cousin Mordecai. Only now did she see them stretching upward into the evening sky.

The king gazed into the distance. "Gallows . . . built to execute Mordecai?" He turned again to glower at Haman, who was being held by two guards. "Take Haman and hang him on his own gallows!" the king coldly ordered without a moment's hesitation.

With quick obedience, the guards dragged Haman away, screaming until his voice faded into the night.

Esther cringed at the suddenness of events. It was all very frightening. She shivered in the cool evening air and pulled a warm shawl around her shoulders. The scarlet garment took the chill off the night, and before long she began to feel warm again inside.

For the first time in weeks, she felt safe. The king had heard her petition. He had been outraged at Haman's treachery toward Esther and her people, and, not surprisingly, had ordered Haman's execution. And yet she was still worried because the death decree was still in effect. Until something was done about that, Esther knew she could never completely rest.

CHAPTER 39

Within the hour, King Xerxes summoned all his royal officials to the court in the citadel. Now that Haman was dead, more decisions needed to be made. Courtiers, counselors, astrologers, and soothsayers of the palace all crowded into the court to witness the latest change of power at the top. With Haman now gone, the royal princes made up a council of six, and with Xerxes that made seven.

The hour was late by the time everyone had arrived, but no one complained. When King Xerxes issued a command, everyone jumped to do his bidding. Esther guessed it was because they had all heard about Haman's hanging, and no one wanted to displease the king.

Esther was asked to stay for the late-night session too. Although she was just an observer, she was given a small throne to one side of the royal dais. She assumed that the king's business at hand concerned her, or she would never have been invited to stay. After all, it was her life and the life of her people that were at risk.

To Esther's surprise, Mordecai was present too. But then he was a royal scribe, so perhaps he was being asked to record the decisions of the meeting.

A courtier stepped forward and raised his hand for silence. "The court of King Xerxes is now in session," he announced ceremoniously. At this, the entire court bowed with their faces to the floor and then stood to hear what the king had to say.

In a commanding voice, the king proclaimed, "Let it be known this day that because of Haman's treachery against my wife, the beautiful Queen Esther, I am giving her the estate of Haman here in Susa. In addition, I'm giving her the deeds to all Haman's property throughout the empire, his livestock, and his wealth in the royal treasury."

King Xerxes looked stern as he sat on his throne in his royal robes of purple, but Esther could see a tired smile playing across the corners of his mouth. Being the most powerful man in the world couldn't be an easy job, she realized.

"And now for a promotion that is well deserved." The king nodded toward Mordecai. "Mordecai, son of Jair, step forward."

Everyone turned in surprise, and none more than Esther. Mordecai's expression revealed his astonishment, but he didn't hesitate long. It wouldn't do to keep King Xerxes waiting. The brave scribe quickly knelt in the presence of the king, his head bowed respectfully.

With great ceremony, the king took his scepter and touched it to Mordecai's left and right shoulders. "Mordecai, faithful scribe of the Persian court!" came the trumpetlike tones. "Zealous to serve your king, courageous in your efforts to stand against the evil Haman, and most important, cousin to my Queen Esther, I now promote you to the position of prime minister in the place of Haman."

A gasp went up from the watching crowd of officials and royal guests. No one had foreseen this promotion, least of all Esther! Mordecai was just a lowly scribe, even if it was a prestigious position at the inner palace gate!

The king took the scribe's hand and raised him to his feet. "Mordecai! On your finger I place the signet ring of this office to give you authority and jurisdiction second only to me." With great solemnity, King Xerxes performed the ceremony. A royal courtier then stepped forward with a diamond-studded box, clasped with golden hinges.

"And this is the royal seal," King Xerxes said, opening the small casket in the courtier's hand. "With it you can write letters of correspondence to all provinces and nations and satrapies throughout the Persian Empire.

"Oh! And one more thing, Mordecai," King Xerxes smiled at Mordecai and then turned to his queen. "I'd like you to manage the estate of the former prime minister and conduct its business according to all that Esther shall ask."

A buzz filled the throne room as the king announced an end to the royal business of the court. The six princes also stood to leave. One by one, they left the court, their retinue of attendants in tow. When the courtroom had finally cleared, Esther remained seated. Only after the king had finished up some business with his court crier and Mordecai did he take the time to notice her.

"What is your pleasure, my lovely queen?" he asked fondly. A lot had happened in the last few days, and he was beginning to see that Esther had helped strengthen his kingdom more than he would have guessed. She had helped uncover a plot to assassinate him and had now helped rid the kingdom of an evil prime minister.

Esther stepped from her throne and knelt on the courtroom floor, putting her face to the red and blue marble surface. She remembered her place in the royal court. Never raise your face to look at the king, keep your head bowed respectfully, and never speak unless spoken to, Hegai had warned her.

"Come," the king said quietly, stretching his golden scepter out to her. "You may speak freely."

Only now did Esther raise her face to accept the king's offer, and this time she dared to make eye contact with the man who was both her husband and a powerful monarch. "If the king regards me with favor and is pleased with me," she began slowly, "and if he thinks it the right thing to do, let an order be written overruling the decree that Haman son of Hammedatha wrote to destroy the Jews in all the king's provinces. For how can I bear to see disaster fall on the Jews? How can I bear to see the destruction of my people?"

The king's face was serious as he contemplated Esther's words. "I'd like to do that, but it won't be that easy, as I'm sure you know. According to Persian law, I cannot override Haman's decree because no document written in the king's name and sealed with his ring can be revoked." King Xerxes continued, "Haman was indeed an evil man! Only a brilliant but evil man could hatch such a plan to destroy the queen and Mordecai and all the Jews in the empire." His eyes grew sad once more as he realized how gullible he had been to allow his prime minister to deceive him.

"If it pleases the king," Mordecai was still standing, but he bowed respectfully, "there might be one other option we can try. We can write another decree in the king's name on behalf of the Jews. We can make it like the first decree, but this time include a statement that allows the Jews to defend themselves against attack."

The king's eyes brightened at this suggestion. "A good solution. Add another section to the decree, Mordecai. I trust you. Make all the necessary arrangements to have the revised decree circulated, and seal it with the king's signet ring."

The king sighed and leaned back on his throne. "Now, Mordecai, I'm tired. Is there anything else I can do for you before I retire for the evening?"

Mordecai got down on his knees before the monarch. "Oh king, live forever! You are gracious indeed to one as lowly as I. However, if it pleases the king, I would like to give credit to a boy who had a major part in bringing your assassinators to justice."

The king sat forward in surprise on his golden throne. "There was someone else whom we should have honored? Why wasn't I informed?"

Mordecai paused, his head still bowed. "I'm sorry, Your Majesty, but at that time none of us was really concerned about who would get credit and which names would be included in the royal records. We were concerned only for your safety, Your Highness."

The king nodded. "Tell me about this boy."

"His name is Arian, and he's a slave in the royal kitchen," Mordecai replied. "He was the one who came to me and told of the conversation he heard between Bigthan and Teresh." Mordecai glanced at Esther. "When he came to me, I sent the details on to the queen."

"What shall we do to reward him?" the king leaned forward again.

"I would like him to be given his freedom, and—and I would like to adopt him as a son in my own household."

A gasp went up from the few who were still in the courtroom, and then the faces broke into smiles.

"So be it," the king sighed again as he rose to go. "Draw up those documents, too, and sign it with my seal. Let it be done as you have said."

CHAPTER 40

The next morning, Mordecai called in all the royal scribes to write up the new decree. It was the twenty-third day in the month of Sivan. The new orders were written to every satrap, governor, and noble in the 127 provinces stretching from India to Ethiopia. They were written in the language of each people, and a special document was even written to the Jews in the Hebrew tongue. Mordecai wrote the orders in the name of King Xerxes, sealed the dispatches with the king's signet ring, and then sent them by mounted couriers.

Esther watched from a balcony in the royal palace as horses, mules, and camels were prepared for the journey. By late afternoon, the messengers had all received their final instructions and were heading out in every direction. Some rode west to the Upper Tigris and Euphrates River Valleys, some south to the ports of the sea, and some east across the mountains to India. Evening and early morning would be the best times to ride. In some cases, special guards would ride with them if they were to travel through hostile territory. It wasn't an easy task, and each courier was reminded of the dangers he might face.

"Please, Lord," Esther prayed, "You know how important the safety of these couriers is. Help them all to reach their destinations safely! Don't let even one be detained along the way. May Your people be delivered, and may Your Name be praised!"

The king's new decree allowed the Jews in every city the right to defend and protect themselves, and if necessary, to kill anyone that might attack them or their wives and children. And surprisingly, the decree even gave the Jews permission to keep the property of the enemies that attacked them. The day when the decree would go into effect was none other than the thirteenth day in the month of Adar.

When the new decree reached its destinations, there was great rejoicing among the Jews, and celebrations were held everywhere in the empire. But nowhere did the Jews celebrate more than in Susa. After all, it was in Susa that God had raised up Queen Esther, a deliverer for her people.

God could choose to protect His people, but they were in a foreign country after all, and they had been warned to return home to Judea long before. In fact, during the previous sixty years, God had inspired three separate decrees to be written by three different Persian kings. The Jews had had plenty of time to take advantage of the opportunities God had given them. They could have escaped the pagan land to which they had been exiled as slaves more than 120 years before, but most had failed to take advantage of the decrees. Most had stayed on in Babylon and Persia. They owned businesses in this foreign land, and family was there. To them, the hardships of traveling back to Judah to make a new start had seemed too difficult, and now, too late they realized that praying to God was their only hope.

Months passed, and as the days and weeks went by, Esther could feel the tension mounting. They spent many days in fasting and prayerful study of the Torah, which had always been the strength of their people. Many an evening, Esther called for Mordecai to lead out in prayer sessions with her and her maidens. Sometimes the prayer sessions asking God for deliverance lasted all night. Meanwhile, Jewish leaders in Susa and the surrounding cities also prayed, and as the thirteenth day of Adar approached, the number of prayer meetings increased.

And then the day finally arrived. Perhaps things turned out well for the Jews because God had blessed them. Perhaps it was the fasting and praying that had made the difference. "The prayer of righteous men and women has great power with God," Mordecai had always said, and the events of the day supported his belief.

On the very day the enemies of the Jews had hoped to overpower them, the tables were now turned. As the fateful day dawned in all the provinces of Persia and Media, the Jews banded together to defend themselves against those who wanted to destroy them.

And the results were absolutely amazing! No one could stand against the Jews. Angels of God were sent as a shield to protect God's people throughout the cities of Persia. Some stories told of battles where mobs of angry thugs tried to attack the homes and meeting places of Jews. Miraculously, swords fell powerless from the hands of evil men, and sooty torches thrown onto rooftops were snuffed out mysteriously. Other tales told of violent thunderstorms forming under clear blue skies. In one case, an earthquake even rocked the foundations of a city, sending gangs of villains scurrying away in every direction.

And when the news spread that the Jews were getting the upper hand over those who hated them, nobles of the provinces, satraps, governors, and the king's administrators began helping the Jews. What else could they do? Mordecai and his God were too much for them. The mighty Haman had dared to stand against Mordecai and Queen Esther, and had failed. What chance did they have against such odds?

And when the long day was finally over, everyone in Susa breathed a sigh of relief. Mordecai's new decree had been a perfect response to Haman's decree, and thousands of Jewish lives were spared. The Jews had counted on God to deliver them, and He had not disappointed them. They were safe at last.

Soon there was feasting, dancing, and music in every section of Susa. At first it was only the Jews who were celebrating, but by the next day, even the Persians began to join in. Everyone was so happy to have the dreadful day behind them.

On the third day, Mordecai finally called in all the officials of the court and made a proclamation to honor Jehovah and King Xerxes. "King Xerxes made this new decree possible," Mordecai declared, "but Jehovah made sure Heaven's angels carried it out." The court officers smiled at Mordecai's humor, but they realized it must be true.

And Queen Esther held a party for her maidens, chamberlains, and palace servants too. It was a wonderful celebration, filled with music and laughter and the best foods the palace chefs could prepare. And the harem wives were invited too. There was great rejoicing up and down the corridors of the palace and out in the garden courtyards of the queen's royal suite.

The celebration feast was so successful that Mordecai and Esther declared it to be a national holiday to be held each year on the fourteenth day in the month of Adar. They even wrote it into law for all generations to come, calling it the Feast of Purim, a time to remember when sorrow and mourning for the Jews was turned into joy. It was all so spontaneous, uplifting, and wonderful! A new era had dawned for the royal household in the palace complex—and for Jews everywhere in the empire.

And to make the holiday even more special, Mordecai commanded that people everywhere should give gift baskets of food to one another and presents to the poor.

And so Mordecai and Esther's power and popularity increased in Susa and throughout the land of Persia. Wherever Mordecai went in his chariot, people congratulated him for saving the life of the king. Wherever Esther went, she was revered and admired for being the most beautiful woman in the kingdom and for standing up against the evil Haman to save her people.

CHAPTER 41

It was a warm spring evening in the month of Nisan when the swallows had returned and sparrows were chirping in the shrubs and vines. Insects were beginning to stir after the cool, rainy winter, and flowers had sprung to life after lying dormant for months.

Esther, Mordecai, and Bithiah were dining in the queen's private garden. Arian was there, too, now officially a son of Mordecai. A new light shone in Mordecai's eyes as he looked with pride on the son he had always wanted, but never had. The boy had even taken Mordecai's family name. He was seventeen now, and although still a boy at heart, he had the honest face of a hard-working young man. His unusual blue eyes were his most charming feature, and a shock of dark hair across his forehead gave him a carefree look.

Esther thought there wasn't a more handsome boy anywhere. It was wonderful to have a new half brother. After all, if she considered Cousin Mordecai to be her father, that made Arian her brother.

The royal meal was elegant but simple. Mordecai liked it that way. Esther had spared no pains in making the meal special, and Droxshana had helped her plan it. Among the delightful foods served were roasted lamb and partridge imported from the hills of Judea.

Droxshana thought it improper that she eat at the table with Esther, Mordecai, and Arian, but Esther would have none of it. "You're the dearest friend I have in the palace," she assured Droxshana. "Of course you'll dine with us."

And so the five of them drank a toast to the honor of Jewish people everywhere. They drank a toast to surviving the ordeal they had all been through since Esther had first come to the royal palace as the new queen of Persia.

Mordecai stared lovingly at his beautiful cousin, not just a girl in his eyes anymore, but a queen of the most powerful kingdom on earth. "Your beauty and sweet disposition can turn any head," he said proudly. "It's no wonder the king made his decision so easily."

"Well, if you hadn't come to care for me when my parents died, I would have never ended up in Susa at all," Esther retorted.

The new prime minister grinned. "Yes, but if it hadn't been for your willingness to approach the king to plead for the Jewish people, we would probably be only history now."

Esther wasn't about to be outdone. "And if you hadn't sent me the warning message about the assassination plot, there would've been no king for me to approach."

"True," Mordecai paused and smiled again as if he had run out of compliments, but then quickly added, "and if it hadn't been for your courage, you wouldn't have dared to confront Haman in the king's presence either."

The other three grinned as the compliments flew back and forth, their eyes flitting from Mordecai to Esther, and back to Mordecai again.

Esther glanced at them and caught the humor of it all, and then she and Mordecai began to laugh. They laughed so hard in fact that tears came to their eyes. Finally, Esther held up her hand as if to catch her breath.

"All right! All right! It's true," she gasped, almost hysterical with the giggles. "We've all had a part in bringing hope and justice and celebration to our people in Susa. Bithiah, Arian, and Droxshana have been a part of it, too, giving us information, advice, and support."

She smiled sweetly at the people with her around the table. "Throughout Persia, the Jewish people are singing our praises for bringing deliverance, but the credit isn't ours. It belongs only to Jehovah, the God of our fathers, the God of Abraham, Isaac, and Jacob. He's the God of all the great deliverers in Hebrew history, such as Moses, Samuel, and David. The great prophets Isaiah, Ezekiel, Jeremiah, and Daniel have all inspired us. They did it through their humble lives of service, and most of them accomplished great things while they were still young. Like Droxshana here and Arian and myself. Sorry Mordecai and Bithiah," she teased.

Mordecai and Bithiah smiled at each other.

"Praise Jehovah for His amazing grace!" Esther closed her eyes as she thought about God's goodness to her and her people. "May future generations read our story as it has been recorded in the annals of the king, and may they give Jehovah the glory He deserves forever and ever!"

In her heart, Esther knew that all five of them at the table would never be the same. They had witnessed some of the most amazing events in Jewish history. They had been tested by trial and treachery and had grown stronger from it. Jehovah, the One True God, the Creator of heaven and earth had once again proved to be their Deliverer!

From this great deliverance, many more Jews were now impressed that they should return to Judea, their homeland. Thousands would eventually make the long journey back to the land of their fathers. But much remained to be done. Reports were coming back that the wall of the Holy City had not yet been rebuilt, and there was no finished temple where the Jews could worship God. And the surrounding nations were also providing opposition that was hampering progress.

Esther wondered whether there was something else she could do. Perhaps she had become queen for several reasons. Surely there were other leaders in the royal court of Persia to whom she could turn for help in making the finished temple and city wall a reality. Time would tell. But this evening she was content to relax in the garden and enjoy the well-deserved rest in the company of those she loved.

IF YOU ENJOYED THIS BOOK, YOU'LL WANT TO READ THESE OTHER BOOKS BY *BRADLEY BOOTH*

Swat bugs with the Egyptians!

Plagues in the Palace

"Enough!" shouted Pharaoh Amenhotep. Meshach had just witnessed the first scene in a drama that would change his life forever. You won't want to put down this exciting story set in the land of Egypt.

160 pages. 0-8163-2143-4

Cross the sea on dry ground!

Escape From Egypt

"The Egyptian Army is coming!" The whole camp was in an uproar. Then Moses' voice boomed out. "Don't worry my people! Jehovah is our Refuge and Fortress."

160 pages. 0-8163-2305-4

Win the war with a slingshot!

Shepherd Warrior

What is it like to go and fight? David wondered as he watched his brothers leave for war against the Philistines. But God knew the plans He had for the young man.

160 pages. 0-8163-2161-2

Journey with the prisoners of war!

Prince of Dreams

Jeremiah's prophecy had come true. Daniel and his friends were prisoners of war, marching in shackles all the way from Jerusalem to Babylon. Could they trust God now?

160 pages. 0-8163-2253-8

Three ways to order:

1 Local	Adventist Book Center®
2 Call	1-800-765-6955
3 Shop	AdventistBookCenter.com

Pacific Press®